The

Star

In the

Mirror

Also by John Bowens

Tropical Illusions

Anybody Could Be Touched

JOHN BOWENS

The

Star

In the

Mirror

STEP YA GAME UP PUBLISHING
URBAN FICTION NEEDS TO BE BELIEVABLE

LIBRARY OF CONGRESS CATALOGING-IN-PUBLICATION
DATA
Bowens, John, author
The Star in the Mirror / John Bowens
p.   cm.
ISBN 978-0-9853303-2-3 (paperback)

The Star in the Mirror

This is a work of fiction. Names, characters, places, and incidents are products of the author's imagination or are used fictitiously. Any resemblance to actual events or locales or persons, living or dead, is entirely coincidental.

DEDICATION:

This book is dedicated to my children. Tamara L. Howell, John Tarik, and Jonivan Emanuel. I Love You!

CHAPTER ONE

He ran! It seemed like the logical thing to do. The cold night air invaded his lungs causing a burning sensation. The dark street he ran down was quiet except for the sound of his Timberland boots hammering against the pavement. Sirens from cop cars getting closer could be heard in the distance, but by far, the sound of his heart racing seemed to be much louder. Peanut was perspiring like a professional boxer after a twelve-round bout.

The headlights of an approaching car startled him as it drove slowly – too slowly – up the deserted street. Moving swiftly, Peanut dipped behind a van. He crouched low and leaned against the cold side of the van's back door, and that's when he noticed it. He was still clutching the snub nose .357 Magnum!

"Peanut?" A voice called out incessantly.

Peanut remained frozen like a picture. Seconds crawled by like minutes as the voice from the creeping car urgently sought his attention. Breathing hard, he waited until he was certain the car was gone before he decided to move again.

Peanut peered around nervously. He was startled when a figure appeared from behind a Dodge truck, two cars to the back of the van in which he sought refuge.

"Peanut?" The person whispered as he came closer.

Peanut quickly spun around and leveled the .357 directly at the intruder's chest.

"Peanut it's me, Kool-Aid! Stop pointing that gun at me!" Peanut reluctantly lowered his weapon and Kool-Aid continued, "Yo! You know you're crazy, right? What the fuck made you start shooting like that?"

Peanut was uncertain of how he should respond. The truth was, he was paranoid.

"Reggie Ransom was coming..." He said between heavy breathing. "I don't trust that nigga! He gives me the creeps!"

Reggie Ransom was a name that could conjure up fear in the hearts of killers! It was rumored that he once killed a baby in front of its parents, and then fed the remains to a pack of vicious pitbulls. This was reason enough why Reggie Ransom was not the one to be played with.

Peanut and Kool-Aid's day started off like any other day. They met up with Big Time and went to hang on Jamaica Avenue. Meeting new bitches and getting as many phone numbers as possible was the mission, and of course, a plethora of 40-ounce bottles of Old English 800 was part of the plan too. They got their drink on and enjoyed themselves hanging in front of the Coliseum which was on 165th street; the brick road. In between time, they did some shopping. Peanut copped a crisp pair of construction Timbs, and a butter soft leather E.C. Jacket by *Exclusively Crystal*. Everything was lovely!

Afterward, the crew split up to shower and get dressed, and by night fall they had met back up on **The Bully;** the Boulevard. It was time for niggaz to get their hustle on!

Peanut had sold an entire $500 pack of nickels of crack, and was well into the second pack when the drama started.

There was a phone booth on 116th Avenue and Sutphin Boulevard, directly in front of Feasters, a mom and pop delicatessen. A hood rat chick named Sabrina was huddled around the phone with four of her girlfriends. They had paged someone and was waiting for the person to call back. Simultaneously, Peanut received a page on his pager which he used for business purposes only, and he was attempting to use the phone.

"Ayo, watch out, I gotta use the phone real quick," Peanut said, pushing one of the girls to the side and grabbing the telephone.

"Don't be pushing me!" The girl exploded.

"You don't see us waiting to use the phone? I'm waiting for a phone call, Peanut!" Sabrina added with attitude.

"Bitch, y'all don't own this phone! Fuck outta here with that bullshit; niggaz is tryna get money." Peanut said, dismissing them.

"Your daughter is a bitch!" Sabrina shot back.

"Fuck that nigga, 'Brina. He gonna get his," one of her friends threatened.

"What?" Peanut yelled, clutching the phone menacingly.

"You heard me, you snitch ass nigga! Everybody knows you got locked up for selling drugs and you was out the same night!"

That statement was enough to get a person in trouble. Peanut dropped the phone and punched shorty right in her mouth! The girl was dazed. Sabrina tried to help her friend, but Peanut had already wrapped her hair around his fist and was flinging her around like a rag doll!

Big Time came out of Feasters and was shocked by what he saw taking place right there on the Ave. He grabbed Peanut and tried to pry him off of her.

"Let her hair go, dawg! That's a female!" Big Time reminded him. He struggled with Peanut while a small crowd began to form.

"Fuck that!" Peanut said before reluctantly letting go of the girl's hair. "She wanna act like a man, she can get her ass beat like a man."

"You got that!" The girl said, looking for her earrings that had fallen during the scuffle. "But you still a snitch. Big Time and Kool-Aid ain't your friends; they know what the fuck you did. Everybody just counting the days for you to get yours! That's right nigga, you saw the movie – I know what you did last summer!"

Peanut lunged at the girl again, but Big Time held him back. "Bitch, you better watch your mouth!" Peanut threatened.

"Sabrina, go 'head yo! Why don't y'all just break the fuck out? I got this!" Big Time pleaded.

The girls gathered their stuff and began moving down the Bully, talking plenty of shit as they left.

Big Time let Peanut go, but Peanut was still furious. He knew he was suspect because of the incident when he got arrested and was released the same night. Nevertheless, he thought the streets had bought his story that he received a desk appearance ticket for loitering. This was the first time he came face to face with what the streets were actually saying.

Peanut shot daggers in the direction that Sabrina and her friends had gone. That's when he saw him! The girls were talking to him, and they were pointing in Peanut's direction.

It was none other than Reggie Ransom!

Peanut was on automatic! He reached into the waist of his jeans and pulled out his hammer. Pointing toward the sky, he squeezed off two shots. As an afterthought, he squeezed off one more. People began to scatter. Some dropped to the ground, and others simply ducked out of fear of being shot.

With Peanut, it didn't take long for instinct to kick in. He ran! It seemed like the logical thing to do.

Now he was crouched down behind a van, still clutching his gun, and the police sirens were getting closer.

"Come on!" Kool-Aid said, cutting between two houses. Peanut was right behind him. They began to maneuver through backyards, jumping fence after fence, while at the same time trying to avoid the yards with dogs.

Suddenly, Peanut's pace slowed. He was dead tired from all the running and began to get cramps.

"Hold up, yo!" He yelled out to Kool-Aid.

Peanut put his gun in his pants pocket and crouched down in the darkness of a yard until the cramps eased up. Kool-Aid doubled back to see what the problem was. "Ayo, whatchu doing???"

"I'm tired... I gotta rest for a minute," Peanut wheezed between deep breaths.

"Where your gun at?" Kool-Aid asked.

"It's in my pocket. Why?"

"Let me see it so I can make sure everything is alright."

An alarm went off in Peanut's head. Kool-Aid was his homie, but this was a strange request.

"What?" Peanut asked, playing dumb.

"I said, let me see your gun, nigga, so I can check the area, make sure that nigga didn't follow us!"

Peanut felt stupid. He was being paranoid. Kool-Aid was his boy, and as such, he knew he could be trusted. He dug inside his pocket and passed Kool-Aid the gun.

"Ayo, Peanut?" Kool-Aid whispered, taking a few steps back. "I need to ask you a question too... Actually, Reggie Ransom wanted me to ask you this, but me personally, I wanna know the answer."

The alarms rang again inside Peanut's head. This time they had him on the verge of a panic attack.

"Wha. . . What the fuck is you talking about, kid?" Peanut stammered, struggling to appear cool.

"You know what I'm talking about, Peanut. Don't make this harder than it already is." Kool-Aid was being sincere. This was really a difficult situation for him.

"Come on, Kool-Aid. We . . .we been friends ever since elementary school. Wha . . .what Reggie Ransom tryin' to put in your head?"

Kool-Aid shook his head in the dark. He watched Peanut closely as he slowly asked him, "Tell me about the star in the mirror?"

When Kool-Aid said those words, Peanut knew it was over. He knew he was going to die. He was almost positive, but he knew he still needed to plead for his life.

"Listen to me, Kool-Aid! This ain't got nothing to do witchu. They, they, they got the streets on lock, and they got eyes and ears everywhere! This is bigger than me and you, man!"

Kool-Aid couldn't believe it and he didn't want to, but Peanut had just confirmed it. Peanut was working with the star in the mirror! For this reason, he had to die.

"I got a daughter, Kool-Aid! Please, homie, don't kill me, man. Please?!"

Kool-Aid shook his head in pity.

"You should've thought about that before you did what you did. Tell Chuck I'll see him when I get there."

"Noooooooooooooo!!!"

Bhop, bhop, bhop!!!

CHAPTER TWO

Detectives John O'Conner and Bill Doherty, also known as Batman and Robin within the urban community, were up to their old tricks again. They were parked on 227th Street, between 115th and 116th Avenues, in the Cambria Heights section of Queens, New York. They were sitting in a gold Lexus LS 430 conducting surveillance on Leroy Green, the head of a major drug operation, who was unfortunate enough to make it on their shit list.

Make no mistake about it, Batman and Robin were some crooked ass cops. In fact, they may have qualified as two of the dirtiest cops in NYPD's history, and they had a network of crooked cops seemingly at their beck and call.

In the past, Internal Affairs launched a barrage of investigations in a futile attempt to bring the duo down, but they accomplished nothing. They did, however, succeed in making both Batman and Robin more cautious. The dirty cops laid low for over a year in one instance, only accepting money from some of their most trusted associates.

There was just one problem: the dirty cops became accustomed to living beyond their means. The thrill of their activities no longer motivated them. There now existed a need to continue their criminal behavior. Batman and Robin made the mistake of allowing themselves to become addicted to the lifestyle. They enjoyed trips to Italy, vacation homes in Florida, college funds for their children, luxury cars for their wives, and all the things that would never have been possible on a policeman's salary.

Then there was the power! The power of making gangsters and thugs submit. The power of doing whatever the hell they chose to do while hiding behind a badge that supposedly represented justice.

It was this power, along with a strong desire to continue living it up, that brought the dynamic duo out of retirement.

Leroy Green was a thirty-something year old heroin dealer who managed to stay under the radar long enough to graduate to the major leagues. A major league player, in the eyes of Batman and Robin, was a person who was smart enough to amass seven figures and better, illegally, without attracting government scrutiny.

Leroy was placed under the microscope after one of his workers stole two kilos of uncut heroin from him, which had the street value of nearly half a million dollars. The worker, who was driving without a license or registration, was also guilty of driving while Black, and was subsequently pulled over for a violation that didn't exist. The police officers conducted an illegal search of the vehicle and found the two keys of heroin on the back seat in a knapsack.

When Leroy Green learned what happened, he was furious! He instructed one of his lieutenants to go to the court house to see how the worker made out. After learning that the worker was being held on a million-dollar bail, Leroy hired a bail bondsman and arranged for the bail to be posted. That same night, after being released, the worker was found dead with a single bullet lodged in his forehead.

That was enough to spark the interest of Batman and Robin. They decided to pay Leroy Green a visit.

Detective John O'Conner was singing, "*We're in the money*" as they trailed behind Leroy's black SUV. They pulled him over about a block away from Forty Projects, on Guy R. Brewer Boulevard and 110th Avenue. Approaching on both sides of the Lincoln Navigator, John O'Conner strategically placed himself on the driver's side since he was deemed the mouthpiece of the duo. He was also the "good guy" when it came time to implement the "good cop/bad cop" routine.

Leroy Green had his driver's license, registration, and insurance ready when John O'Conner approached the window.

"Black, I'm not interested in your paperwork. Step out of the vehicle, I need to have a word with you," Detective O'Conner said, peering into the back of the SUV.

Leroy, A.K.A. Black, was skeptical, and it showed on his face. This cop just addressed him by his nickname, wasn't interested in his paperwork, and wanted him to step out of his truck? Black knew better than that!

"Have a word with me about what? My paperwork is legit, I'm not in violation of any—"

"Shut the fuck up and get out of the truck before I find a gun on your passenger seat!" Bill Doherty snapped, coming around the truck. "And if you really piss me off, I might even find a couple of ounces of crack cocaine in the glove compartment."

"That won't be necessary, Bill." John said. He tapped on the driver side door. "Come on Black, hop out. I'll explain everything to you on the sidewalk. Give me two minutes. I promise you, arresting you is the last thing on my mind."

Reluctantly, Leroy Green jumped out of his truck and met John O'Conner in front of a laundromat. A lady with an old scarf on her head like Aunt Jemima was inside the laundromat washing clothes. She seemed to be the only one who was curious as to what was going on.

Black glanced at his watch impatiently and cleared his throat. "Did I run a red light or something?"

"No Black, we're actually interested in your thriving heroin business," John O'Conner said, rubbing his hands together quickly and getting straight to the point.

Black tried to maintain a poker face, but he wasn't disciplined enough. His expression was one of amazement.

"If I may be candid," John continued, "You've become a shark in the pond. The good news is that the big boys don't even recognize you as a major player, you're under the radar. That's the way I would like to keep it, Black, but anonymity comes with a price." He paused to let his words sink in. "Black, I want to do business with you—"

"Listen Officer," Black said sarcastically, cutting John off. "I don't have the slightest idea what you're talking about. I'm a businessman, a LEGIT businessman. I own two barber shops and a sneaker store, and that's where it ends."
"Leroy, don't be so hasty. I can get kilos of high quality drugs to you for good prices. I can get you

14

guns. Hell, you won't even need guns—I can protect you! My price for these services would be about—"

"You got the wrong man! I'm sorry, but you got the wrong man, Officer."

"Nigger, do you know who you're fucking with?!" Bill interjected.

John put a hand on Bill's chest in a mock attempt at holding the big fella back. "Take it easy, Bill," he coached, then returned his attention to Leroy. "I just want you to think about it, Black. Please?"

"There's nothing to think about," Black said dismissively.

"Are you sure?"

"I'm positive."

"Well, thanks for your time."

"You better watch your back!" Bill yelled.

"Yeah, whatever," Black shot back.

That's how Leroy Green made it on the shit list.

Now Batman and Robin were parked on a quiet block in Queens with diabolical intentions. If Leroy Green didn't want to play ball, it was fine with them. There was going to be a game, one way or another.

Through high powered binoculars they watched the house that they suspected Black used to stash either cash or drugs, hopefully both. Stanley and Tom were parked further up the block as a safety precaution just in case something jumped off.

"I think we have some activity," John informed his partner as he observed the grey station wagon pull up in front of the stash house.

Darren Johnson, A.K.A. DJ, and his girlfriend Kim exited the grey station wagon and made their way up the walkway leading to the house.

"Good things come to those who wait!" Bill sang as he stared through his binoculars. "If I'm not mistaken, that's our boy, DJ!"

When DJ and Kim made it to the front door of the stash house, they both looked up simultaneously. They were talking to someone in the second-floor window when a set of keys were thrown down. Kim used the keys to unlock the front door, while DJ doubled back to the car and retrieved a huge green duffle bag.

John O'Conner's heart skipped a beat as he reached for his two-way radio. "Stanley, you guys be alert! This may be it!" he said, salivating over the mic.

Batman and Robin had followed Leroy Green on half a dozen occasions, but this was the second time they found themselves at this particular house. On both occasions, Black circled the block two times before declaring the house safe to approach. The detectives were used to playing cat and mouse, and now their patience was paying off. After sitting in a parked car for two and half hours, drinking coffee and eating donuts, their time had arrived.

DJ lugged the green duffle bag through the front door of the house and then returned to the station wagon for a second trip. John O'Conner almost came in his pants.

"Back me up!" He yelled into his radio. He turned to his partner, "Let's go!"

They departed the Lexus, slamming the doors. They ran across front lawns, simultaneously drawing their guns. Mid-stride, John reached into his shirt and retrieved his badge which hung from a chain around his neck.

Before DJ knew what the hell was happening, they had the drop on him.

"Freeze asshole! Make a move and you're dead!"

Bill got a hold of DJ and John grabbed the bag. Stanley and Tom pulled up in a burgundy Ford Taurus and double parked in front of the house. They exited their vehicle with guns drawn. Using the training they received to preserve justice, they entered the stash house.

Inside, Kim ran around the house frantically. "It's a raid! The cops are outside!" She screamed.

Bill forced DJ inside the house and made him lay on the floor. Tom found Kim inside the kitchen and brought her to lay with her boyfriend, while Stanley followed John to the second floor in a tactical formation.

The sound of the toilet flushing repeatedly could be heard as they reached the second-floor landing. The detectives paused on either side of the door and gathered themselves. With his gun leveled, John spun into the bathroom only to find Leroy Green attempting to dump pounds of heroin down the toilet. It was a funny sight, really. Black with a coat of heroin dust all over his face and body, wearing a look on his face as if he had just got caught masturbating.

"We meet again," John said with a smirk. Meanwhile, Stanley cleared the remainder of the house.

When they brought Black downstairs to lay beside his co-defendants, Tom shared the discovery of what was inside the duffle bags. Everyone thought it was drugs, but both bags turned out to be filled with money. Fives, tens, twenty's, and fifty's – all drug money!

"Well, Leroy," John began with a smirk. "I have good news and bad news. Which do you want to hear first?"

When it became evident that Black didn't intend to answer the question, Bill offered some assistance.

"Hell, I want to hear the good news!"

"The good news, Bill? Well, the good news is that I'm not going to lock his black ass up. That's the good news."

"So, what's the bad news?" Bill asked sarcastically.

"Oh, the bad news is that I'm taking all of this money."

"And the drugs, don't forget the drugs," Tom added.

"Yes, of course! And the drugs. We have to take the drugs, what's left of it anyway. Leroy was trying to flush perfectly good drugs down the toilet. Can you believe that?" John said. "A word to the wise, Black. The next time you get on your feet, if you're able to do so, do us both a favor and show a little bit more respect when I pay you a visit."

$$$

Stanley Kavoski was a pedophile. Tom Kramer was unaware of this, and Batman and Robin were certainly in the dark concerning this matter. Unfortunately, Internal Affairs was very familiar with the dirty deeds that Stanley would prefer to be left in the closet. Stanley was, in fact, caught red handed pursuing his sickness as he communicated with a Federal Agent on the internet posing as a 12-year-old boy. He attempted to rendezvous with the child in his car a block away from the elementary school that he thought the child was attending. When Federal Agents surrounded his car, Stanley broke down in tears and pleaded for help.

Stanley Kavoski was in a lot of trouble, so Internal Affairs decided to give him a chance to help himself. Internal Affairs were interested in two individuals.

Batman and Robin.

Stanley wasn't a part of Batman and Robin's network. In fact, Batman and Robin didn't even trust Stanley. However, Stanley was friends with Tom Kramer; they had gone through the academy together. Tom was the one who convinced John O'Conner that Stanley would be a great back up to replace his regular partner who was recovering from a hernia. Tom insisted that they use Stanley on the Leroy Green mission. He even refused to work with anyone else.

What Tom Kramer couldn't have known was that Stanley was wearing a wire. He was also wearing a tracking device, and when they arrived at Bill Doherty's house out on Long Island to divide the money, a team of Federal Agents arrived shortly after. John O'Conner, Bill Doherty, and Tom Kramer were quickly whisked away in handcuffs.

The infamous Batman and Robin were down for the count, and their network of crooked cops were sure to follow.

Harry Copeland, the commissioner of the Federal Bureau of Investigations, was a fair guy. He was willing to give John O'Conner and Bill Doherty a chance to help themselves.

"Listen guys," Harry said in their first debriefing. "Let's not make this any harder than it already is. You guys have families, we don't want to drag them into this. There's been enough embarrassment. Help me out here. I guarantee you little to no jail time if you cooperate, but you have to give me something I can work with. Come on, let's get the ball rolling."

John O'Conner had always been the spokesman of the two, and after being processed and sitting in that cold ass cell for hours, he was dying to talk.

"What do you want to know?"

Harry Copeland smiled and nodded his head.

"Good. Let's start with Anthony Orena. Tell me everything you know about Anthony Orena."

CHAPTER THREE

The Metropolitan Detention Center in Brooklyn, also known as MDC Brooklyn, is a temporary home to a spectrum of America's worse criminals. In it you'll find prisoners accused of a plethora of crimes, figuratively (and sometimes literally) fighting for their lives.

In a system that ironically claims that the people are innocent until proven guilty, we have thousands of untried men and women who are being deprived of their social rights, and treated as if they've already been convicted of a crime.

Ultimately, a vast majority of these people are railroaded and found guilty of some crime or another, but there still exist a few instances where the people are found innocent.

Jerry Moore was one of the prisoners in MDC who awaited to be tried by the United States Government, only the perception was that he was guilty until proven innocent. He was stripped of his rights, locked in a small cell, and allotted insufficient time and resources to prepare a defense for his case. On top of all this, Jerry Moore was confined to a wheelchair.

The facts be what they may, Jerry Moore wasn't in the business of throwing pity parties. He found no time to feel sorry for himself. This fool was a soldier, and a soldier's sole purpose was to fight.

It was a Monday morning and Jerry Moore awoke to find himself still locked into a living nightmare. He was in a handicap cell, on I-63 unit, feeling like the lower half of his body was weighted down to the mattress. He took his fist and banged against the top bunk of the bunk bed to see if his celly was still in bed. His celly was an old head named Barkim that he knew from United States Penitentiary, Canaan, where he served time on a previous bid. Barkim was a stand-up dude, meaning, he didn't snitch. In the Federal system, snitches were referred to as *hot* dudes. If a person was labeled as being *hot* they generally became outcast from the men who stood up in the face of adversity. In extreme cases, *hot* dudes were attacked and sometimes killed, and thus removed from shark-infested waters.

Jerry Moore propped himself up on his elbows and debated whether he should holla for help, or attempt to get in his wheelchair on his own. There were plaster casts on both the Big Homie's legs. Being the soldier that he was, he opted for the latter. He lifted himself all the way up until he was in a sitting position, and then stopped to figure out what to do next.

Allowing his left hand to serve as a support on the bed, he used his right hand to lift his left leg and swung it over the edge of the bed. With the left leg hanging over the edge, he came back for the right leg, moving it as much as he could to the edge of the bed. Jerry Moore found himself in an awkward position. He needed to move his left leg over some more to make room for his right leg. As he leaned over attempting to move his left leg, The Big Homie lost balance and went crashing to the floor! A sharp pain shot from his legs, but Jerry Moore was more embarrassed than anything else.

He lay on the cold floor looking around for help. After huffing and puffing for a few minutes, he stretched his body over to his locker and grabbed his combination lock. The Big Homie had no need to lock his locker because no one would be stupid enough to steal from him, not even in his present condition. Still, all soldiers were smart enough to buy a lock because a combination lock was a nice weapon. It could be used in numerous ways, but the most common way was to place the lock in a sock. In this instance, the lock was helpful to Jerry Moore because he needed to get someone's attention. He took the lock and threw it at his cell door as hard as he could, creating a loud bang. His celly, Barkim, came, looked in the cell, and found Jerry Moore on the floor.

"Damn Homie, my bad!" Barkim said, rushing to his aid, and helping him into his wheelchair. "I shouldn't have left the cell until you woke up."

"I'm alright, fool!" Jerry Moore said, as if he wasn't just stranded on the floor.

"You gotta use the bathroom?" Barkim asked with concern.

"Nah, just give me a few minutes to take a bird bath and brush my teeth and shit."

"Alright, take care of your business," Barkim said, grabbing his Walkman and leaving the cell.

Jerry Moore rolled his wheelchair by the sink in his cell and peeled off his t-shirt. Across his chest were more reminders that somebody had tried to kill his ass. Two long, nasty cuts bubbled as they healed across his chest. These wounds were inflicted by the same person who had broken his legs, and the scars would last a lifetime.

Jerry Moore turned on the water and took care of his hygiene. Three days out of the week he had to go to medical to have the nurses bath him, and make sure that he was okay. At first, Jerry Moore was embarrassed by the routine. Now, it was something he looked forward to, being that a few of the nurses were very attractive and rubbed him the right way. On the days that he didn't go to medical, he would just take a bird bath like he was doing now.

By the time he got himself together it was almost ten o'clock in the morning. The Big Homie wheeled himself out of the cell. The units in MDC Brooklyn had the capacity to hold up to 120 prisoners. There were two levels on each unit and the cells were situated around the form of a horse shoe. In between the cells was the common area. This space consisted of tables where the inmates ate their meals and played cards, or any of the other available recreational games. There were four 27-inch color televisions in this area that could only be heard through the prisoners' radios. Each television had a station it was programmed to on the radio, and the prisoner would tune in to whichever television he wished to view. There was also a ping pong table and an outside recreational deck that could be accessed from within the unit, for those who wished to play basketball, handball, or just walk and get some fresh air.

There was also a television room on the lower level for people who didn't have a radio. Two of the walls of this room were made of glass, allowing those outside the room to see inside. And there was an exercise room on the second level, right above the T.V. room.

There was a total of 10 individual showers; five on the lower level and five on the upper level.

Half the unit was still sleep at ten in the morning, but there were a few games of chess being played, and a small crowd of inmates seemed to be mesmerized while watching BET. Some of the older prisoners sat by themselves reading newspapers as they enjoyed their second and third cups of coffee.

Jerry Moore wheeled himself over near the television that was in front of his cell. A young kid was standing there watching a video on BET.

"Bay-boy, turn that to CNN," The Big Homie instructed.

The kid took his headphones off his ears so he could hear what Jerry Moore said. "Main man, what you say?" He asked.

"I said, turn to CNN so we can see what's going on in the news."

"I'm watching videos, yo!" The kid barked.

Jerry Moore's co-defendant, Shan Will, was already on his way over after spotting that the Big Homie was out of his cell.

"Niggaz got BET on three T.V.'s, son! I'm trying to see the news," Jerry Moore spit belligerently.

"Why you coming to me? Why you didn't ask them to turn that T.V?"

Ole' boy was giving Jerry Moore a hard time and Shan Will wasn't having it. On automatic, Shan

Will snuffed the kid! The kid fell back in a daze and Shan Will was on him, throwing a barrage of punches. When he finished his attack, the kid lay crumpled on the floor.

Jerry Moore's celly was on the recreational deck. Someone told him something was poppin' off and he ran into the unit.

"What's up, Homie?" Barkim asked, looking from Jerry Moore to Shan Will.

"This bitch ass nigga was talking fly out the mouth to the Big Homie," Shan Will explained, breathing hard.

"I was not," the kid denied, sitting up on the floor. "I just said –"

"Shut the fuck up, I ain't talking to you!" Shan Will said, going at the kid again.

Barkim grabbed the little Homie and held him back.

"Chill Homie, before one of these hot-ass niggas start telling," Barkim reasoned.

"I know these niggaz better watch they mouth," Shan Will said, standing up on a chair and changing the T.V. to CNN.

Jerry Moore tuned his radio to the T.V. so he could listen to the news. Some of the older prisoners went to get their radios so they could check the news too. The younger prisoners were so wild that most of the older guys stayed out of their way to avoid confrontation.

"Barkim, tell Shorty to come 'ere," Jerry Moore said pushing his headphones behind one of his ears.

Barkim went to the kid's cell to fetch him. He found him in the mirror looking at his face.

"Dwayne, my Homie wanna talk to you. Come see what he want and cut that bullshit out."

"I wasn't even on no bullshit, I was just watching videos," Dwayne said, as he began walking over to where Jerry Moore was.

"Just chill out and see what he has to say," Barkim advised.

Jerry Moore was watching as shorty approached. His plan was to feel dude out to see if he wanted some get back, or if he planned on reporting the incident to a staff member.

"You alright, son?" The Big Homie asked as if he was sincere.

"Yeah, I'm straight," Dwayne responded, begrudgingly.

"You sure?" Jerry Moore asked, amused.

Dwayne didn't know why this guy in a wheelchair, who was the cause of him just getting his ass kicked, was now concerned about his well-being.

"Yeah, I'm sure," he insisted.

"That's what's up," Jerry Moore said, nodding his head. "Do you know who I am, Shorty?"

Dwayne was tired of the 21 questions so he just shook his head from side to side.

"Do you know who Jerry Moore is?"

This question got Dwayne's attention.

"One of the Big Homies from Nine Trey gangsters? Jerry Moore and Chandar?" He asked, as if they were on the same page now.

"Yeah, yeah!" Jerry Moore said with a smile. He appreciated the fact that the kid knew who he was, by name at least. "I be that nigga, Jerry Moore!"

Dwayne's eyes almost popped open as wide as saucer plates. "You're serious? You're the one that had the city screaming Sex, Money, Murder???"

Jerry Moore chuckled, "That be me, Bay-boy."

"Damn, that's my bad Big Homie. I didn't know," Dwayne said, nearly bowing his head in shame.

"That shit ain't about nothing. Shan Will, y'all niggaz leave Shorty alone!" Jerry Moore ordered. "What's your name, son?"

"Dwayne."

Jerry Moore stuck his hand out and Dwayne gripped it tight. They shook on it.

"You ain't hot or nothing?" Jerry Moore inquired, letting the question hang.

"Nah, I ain't telling on nobody. All I got is a gun charge."

The Big Homie was about to interrogate the kid to find out exactly who he was dealing with when the unit officer called his name.

"Moore! Jerry Moore, you have an attorney visit."

The C.O. was a skinny brown-skinned chick named Ms. Thomas. Shorty was a little cutie, but she acted like she didn't recognize the Big Homie's status.

Jerry Moore wheeled himself over to the Officer's station.

"You got your I.D. card?" She asked.

Jerry Moore flashed his red inmate I.D. card and Ms. Thomas led him to the front door of the unit. The Big Homie noticed for the first time that ole' girl had a small patch of hair on her neck. She smelled good like a mafucka, but for some reason that patch of hair was a complete turn off!

"This bitch need to either shave that shit off or put some deodorant on her neck!" The Big Homie thought as he rolled out the door.

When Jerry Moore got off elevator, he was escorted to a room that was tucked away from the visiting room. This room was supposed to assure privacy between attorneys and their clients. However, Jerry Moore's lawyer was nowhere in sight. Instead, a hot wings entrée, potato chips, and a soda awaited him in the room.

"You got something to snack on, I guess he'll be right back," the Officer said before leaving Jerry Moore alone in the room.

Jerry Moore had spoken to Kevin Cohen just the day before and the attorney said nothing about coming for a visit. The Big Homie just hoped it was some good news. All the stuff he'd been through, he was due for some good news. He cracked open the hot wings and began punishing them. He had demolished the entrée and was chilling when a man who was not Kevin Cohen entered the room carrying a brief case.

"I'm glad you enjoyed the food, Mr. Moore," the man said taking a seat. "My name is Anthony Bennett, I work with the Assistant U.S. Attorney assigned to your case."

Jerry Moore felt as if he'd been bamboozled. He wanted to regurgitate the food he had just eaten and get as far away from this man as possible.

"Where's my lawyer?" Jerry Moore asked, hoping at least Mr. Cohen was in the building.

"My office has been trying to contact your attorney all morning, to no avail—"

"What the fuck kinda games are you people playing???" The Big Homie growled, skipping the bullshit.

"Listen Jerry, I know you're a soldier. I just want to talk to you, if you feel –"

"Are you gonna answer my question? What kinda games are y'all playing? Y'all know who I am! Y'all know I'm not a snitch! And y'all know I have a right to an attorney!" Jerry Moore's voice echoed off the walls.

Mr. Bennett allowed Jerry to release his venom before he attempted to speak again.

"You have every right to be upset Jerry. If you're found guilty the prosecutor is going to seek the death penalty... your best-case scenario is a Life sentence. I just came to talk to you to see if—"

"I'm out! I don't gotta listen to this bullshit!"

Jerry Moore spun his wheelchair around and rolled toward the door. Mr. Bennett came from behind him and held the wheelchair.

"Just one thing, *Big Homie*! You better hope your co-defendants have balls as big as yours because if they don't – and I'm telling you they don't – there's going to be a line of people longer than the Mississippi River waiting to testify against you. You can stop a killer and save yourself, Jerry. Give us Reggie Ransom! You give us Reggie Ransom and I'll guarantee you a 30-year sentence. That man is an animal. Help us get him off the streets!"

Jerry Moore was steaming as he sat there in his wheelchair, helpless. Anthony Bennett was waiting for a response. He hoped to appeal to the Big

Homie's conscious, but he was in for a rude awakening.

Jerry Moore looked over his shoulder and through gritted teeth, said, "If you don't let go of my muthafuckin' wheelchair..."

CHAPTER FOUR

"Nigga, put your hands where I can see' em!" The deep gravelly voice commanded.

It was pitch black, and Jeff White struggled to see a feature to help him identify this stranger in the night. Two things quickly became painfully evident as Jeff's mind made haste to come up with a plan. One, the stranger was wearing a ski mask. Two, he was clutching a chrome hand gun.

His heart racing, Jeff White took small steps backwards with both hands suspended in front of him. The small black rocks under his feet made a crunching sound with each step.

Crunch... crunch...

They were atop a building somewhere and Jeff White was faced with a dilemma: go out with a fight, or lay down and die. Before Jeff could decide what to do, powerful hands gripped his shirt and he was lifted off his feet. Jeff tried to put up a struggle, but he was no match. His attacker flung him over the ledge as if he was a rag doll.

Jeff was falling! Everything was passing by so quickly! This was it, the big day. He always wondered how he would die and now the time had come. Just before he hit the ground, Jeff White let out a loud cry!

"Ahhhhhhhhhh!!!"

"Nigga, what the fuck is wrong witchu?" Makavelli yelled.

Everyone in the room was looking at Jeff White as if he lost his mind. Jeff sat up on the love seat, he was breathing hard and drenched in sweat. The C.E.O. of Colossal Publishing was mortified! He turned to the only person in the room that he considered a friend and offered an explanation.

"I thought I was gonna die, Shawty! I keep having this dream... ever since I got shot, I be having this dream that a nigga be laying in the cut on me. This time it felt real. I thought I was gonna die! You ever felt like that, Shawty? Like you're about to die? Can you imagine how it feels to think you're about to die?"

Jeff White asked this question with such seriousness that, not only could it be detected in his voice, but you could see it in his eyes. Shawty was spooked! And he wanted to know if his friend could relate.

Wild Blood, Infra-red, and Makavelli watched as Chandar digested the question.

Can you imagine how it feels to think you're about to die?

Chandar's mind immediately recalled the flirt with death that he and A-Blood recently experienced in Anthony Orena's private jet. The thought alone caused the hair to stand up on the back of his neck.

The Galaxy Intercontinental Business Jet had been sabotaged, and somewhere above the State of Ohio the power had shut down and the jet took a nosedive. Gripping the seat as the jet plunged toward the ground, Chandar was certain he was about to die! He was scared. His heart raced, he perspired, and deep down he wanted to cry out, the same way Jeff did. But he didn't. The Big Homie had kept his cool.

As fate would have it, the power was restored, and the pilots were able to regain control of the small plane.

"I know exactly how it feels, Playboy." Chandar responded softly. He was definitely able to empathize.

"I know one thing," Makavelli stated. "He got one more time to do all dat yelling and –"

"Nigga, won't you chill the fuck out!" Chandar interjected.

"Dawg, that nigga scared the shit out of me!" Makavelli protested.

"Just let it go. Matter of fact, don't y'all fools need to be getting ready? The limo will be here to pick us up in about an hour. Get y'all dusty asses in the shower and get dressed so we don't be late for this wedding. That goes for you too Jeff, we don't duck that water," Chandar said trying to lighten up the situation.

Jeff White was humble, but there was no doubt about it that the man would kill if he was forced to. Chandar didn't need him and Makavelli bumping heads

"You need to convey that to Wild Blood. That fool is like the little nigga Pig Pen from Charlie Brown," Infra-red said, palming Wild Blood's head.

"Get off me, fool!" Wild Blood said, snatching his head away and throwing a combination of shadow punches to Infra-red's body.

Satisfied that everything was under control, Chandar spun off to the master bedroom suite. They were in a two-story penthouse down in Miami for Del Gibson's wedding, which was to take place at the Marquis on Biscayne Boulevard. Afterward, the 260-foot yacht *Attessa* would serve as the setting for the wedding's reception.

To kill some time and relieve some stress, Chandar decided to hit the exercise room before he showered. He began a slow jog on the treadmill and zoned out as Nas's classic *Illmatic* flowed from the sound system.

So much was going on! Karen was in New York, seven months pregnant, so Chandar had to prepare to be a father again. That wouldn't be a problem because he loved children. He already had a daughter, Jasmine. She was eight years old and Chandar loved her with every breath in his body. Still, the ghetto star knew he didn't spend nearly enough time with his Princess. Sure, she wanted for nothing, but money could never buy, nor be a substitute for genuine love.

Whenever Chandar thought about his daughter, thoughts of Lisa were never far away. Lisa was his daughter's mother. She was killed in a kidnaping that went terribly wrong. That was years ago, but that still didn't stop him from missing Lisa.

Thinking of Lisa caused a chain reaction, and now thoughts of A-Blood invaded the Big Homie's mind, causing him to quicken his pace on the treadmill.

Chandar hadn't seen or spoken to A-Blood since A-Blood revealed that he was partly responsible for Lisa's death. That news left Chandar devastated.

When the pilots regained control of the Jet that day they were forced to make an emergency landing in Detroit. Chandar was so upset that he left A-Blood right there at the airport without saying a word to him.

Chandar had vowed to kill the person responsible for Lisa's death, but damn, A-Blood??? A-Blood was like family! Truth was, the only thing A-Blood was guilty of was being negligent. A-Blood made a mistake. Bottom line. This was a sensitive matter and it needed to be handled with intelligence, not emotions. It was a possibility that A-Blood would be forgiven. Only time would tell.

Chandar was soaking wet as he perspired profusely. The sweat was burning his eyes but he pushed on. He wiped at his face in a futile attempt at removing the sweat. He picked up his pace on the treadmill as he tried to clear his thoughts, to no avail. His thoughts shifted to another person.

Jerry Moore.

Whoa! This motherfucker successfully defeated the U.S. Government. He gave back a 30-year prison sentence, for what??? Now again, he was trapped in a detention center in Brooklyn, this time with two broken legs.

Jerry Moore caused a great deal of pain to Chandar.

Now Chandar was down in M-I-A for Del Gibson's wedding. Del Gibson, aka Dr. Hyde, was actually a good friend of A-Blood. Chandar had met him personally once and they remained cordial ever since. The ghetto star thought about declining the invitation, but Dr. Hyde was persistent. He insisted that Chandar attend his wedding, and he hinted at an important announcement that would be made at the reception that may be of his interest. That was enough to spark Chandar's curiosity. That, and the fact that A-Blood was out of the country and unable to attend the wedding, pushed Chandar to accept the invitation.

Exhausted, Chandar glided off the treadmill and hit the shower. The steaming hot water gushing from the shower head proved to be invigorating and Chandar cherished the moment.

The life of a shot caller wasn't all that it appeared to be on the surface. You had to be prepared to take the bitter with the sweet. Music videos portrayed a life of platinum and diamonds, luxurious cars and homes, and an abundance of exotic women, but without a proper means of acquiring massive income, we should understand the flip side of the game. No one can fathom a Life sentence in prison until it becomes their reality. No one wants to accept the vision of themselves under six feet of earth, alone, in darkness, separated from the wealth that they worked so hard to acquire. That's when it's too late, and the people ask themselves: was it worth it?

Was it worth it?

When Chandar stepped out of the shower he left these thoughts behind. It was time to put on his game face! He quickly draped himself in a black tailored Tuxedo and slipped into a pair of black suede Gucci shoes. After carefully examining himself in the full mirror, he stepped outside on the balcony and encountered a scene reminiscent of the movie S*carface*. Just as Tony had watched the blimp floating by displaying his message: **The world is yours**, Chandar looked out into the Atlantic Ocean just in time to witness a group of small jets clearly sketching his own message across the sky. The words. . . **What goes up, must come down.**

Chandar shook his head in disappointment. This shit was crazy. He had anticipated a motivational message, not a maxim. As he pondered on the words in the sky, Infra-red came to inform him that the limousine was downstairs. Chandar smiled at his homie.

44

"Let's paint the town red then, Playboy!" Chandar said, slapping his palms together. He was doing a masterful job masking the way he really felt.

The truth was, Chandar was stressed the fuck out!

CHAPTER FIVE

There's a void in the downtown Manhattan skyline in New York City. It used to be such a beautiful scene at any time of the day or night, but now it was different. Still beautiful, but ... different.

This is what Teddy was thinking as he and his man Mike were chillin' atop the roof of building five in Baisley Projects about to blaze some weed.

"I can't believe them shits are gone," Teddy said, staring out into the horizon.

Mike was dumping weed into a gutted cigar. "What shit, son? You can't believe what shit is gone?"

"The World Trade Center," Teddy replied.

This nigga sounded sad as if 9/11 was yesterday as opposed to a year ago.

"Oh," Mike said. He fired up the blunt and inhaled deeply. "I can't believe that shit either. I told you my mom's predicted that shit, right?"

This nigga Mike was bugged out! Teddy cut his eyes at Mike and twisted his mouth.

"Nah, for real, son!" Mike exclaimed, noticing the look on his friend's face. "My mom's is psychic, like Dionne Warwick and shit. It was about a year before that shit happened she told me. She said, 'son... one of these days somebody gonna fly a plane into one of these big ole' buildings.' I said, Momma you crazy, you so crazy!"

Mike took two consecutive drags on the blunt and passed it to Teddy. Teddy couldn't believe that Mike was joking about something so tragic. But then again, this was Mike. This dude would snap jokes at a funeral.

Teddy dismissed the bullshit Mike was talking and proceeded to speak his mind – after hitting the blunt of course.

"New York ain't even the same without the Twin Towers . . . they destroyed a landmark. The fucked-up part is that I wouldn't even care if they blew up the White House. The Pentagon was fair game, but the World Trade Center??? It was nothing but civilians in there. This is America; nine times out of ten, they had Muslims in them buildings. I don't understand that shit!"

Teddy was getting emotional but he figured it was just the weed. He hit the blunt again and went into a coughing fit. Mike was staring at him all stupid.

Of course, the comedian had a comeback.

"You gonna think I'm one of Bin Laden cousins and shit if you don't pass that blunt. I'll blow *this* muthafucka up!" He sang like he was a damn fool. He reminded Teddy of Chris Tucker's character in the movie *Friday*.

Teddy just shook his head and passed the blunt.

"You think everything is a joke. My sister was three blocks away from that shit when it popped off. She had to run across the Brooklyn Bridge!"

"Man, you starting to depress me with this shit, why don't you chill the fuck out and enjoy the high? I'm not mad at Abdullah and them, those fools are like our cousins—they the new niggas. They call them sand niggas. This country been bombing them niggas for the longest. You didn't hear them crying. Everybody paying attention now because that shit hit home. I'm not trying to hear all that bullshit."

Mike was hilarious. He was actually an intelligent guy, he just stayed on joke time, all the time, as if he was trying to escape reality. Teddy recognized what Mike said as the truth, but he didn't comment. Instead, he got lost in thought of how America terrorized every people they encountered. America was built on rape, murder, and deception, but even that paled in comparison to the attack the American government launched against Japan. Teddy knew that Hiroshima was terrorism to the tenth degree! He had read an interview by Marcel Junod, a representative of the Red Cross. In the article, the Japanese man reported the frightening reality of the explosion:

'And suddenly there appeared these intense, pinkish lights, accompanied by an unnatural tremor. This was immediately followed by a wave of heat and violent winds that ravaged everything in its path..." The man recalled. 'In only a few seconds, thousands of people who walked the roads or sat in the city's main streets were burned alive. A great number were killed by the intense heat that spread all over. Others were left lying on the ground screaming in pain with deadly burns all over their bodies. Trains were lifted off the ground along with their tracks as if they were mere toys. Horses, dogs, and livestock were all befallen with what befell the people. Every living thing had lost its life in one painful turn of events too difficult to describe.'

Teddy and Mike finished their blunt and left from atop the roof. They didn't plan to be there if the cops decided to pop up there.

Teddy was high as shit and had the munchies, but Mike suggested they go to the phone booth to call some honies. Needless to say, the honies proved to be more enticing than the munchies.

While they were on their way to the phone booth, a slick ass S500 Mercedes Benz drove by with the music bumping. Alicia Keys' strong vocals poured from the cracked windows and penetrated their ears, 'I keep on falling, innnn and out of love...'

"That's my shit!" Mike yelled. "That's my muthafuckin' song, Teddy. I wish we was rolling like that, in a tight ass Benz sitting on chrome listening to Alicia muthafuckin' Keys."

Mike was being dramatic. Teddy smiled from ear to ear, not just because Mike was a funny dude, but because he felt the same way. He wished they could roll like that.

The way it happened was crazy. Mike called some shorties from Queens Village and set something up for the night. They were walking back to the building when a gold CLS 500 Mercedes pulled up to the curb. The passenger window glided down and Teddy and Mike started bugging because that same Alicia Keys joint was bangin' from the system. That wasn't too amazing though because that song was hot. What was amazing was the person in the driver's seat. It was Teddy's twin brother, Eddie!

"What's up, y'all? What's popping?" Eddie said, getting out of the whip and walking with a swagger.

"Oh my god! No this nigga didn't!" Mike said giving Eddie dap.

"Whose car you got?" Teddy asked, smiling.

"This that nigga Big Time car. I told you he wanna fuck with us. He wanna put work on 112th badder than a mafucka, so he let me hold the whip for the day."

"Word??? We might have to fuck with that nigga then!" Mike said with his hands reaching for the sky. "This nigga shit is phat to death! All that's missing now is some bad ass bitches. What's up kid, what you tryna get into?"

"You already know! It's whatever with me, I just gotta make one stop before we get into anything."

Next thing you know, they were jumping in the Benz and moving like grown men. Mike's stunting ass jumped in the front with Eddie, so Teddy played the back, but he wasn't sweating that. They was rolling in what the streets was calling the four-door coupe—who had a right to complain?

Teddy felt crazy good as they drove through the hood, it felt as if they were floating. Almost everyone they passed damn near broke their necks looking at the car and trying to see who was in it.

Eddie drove to 109th and Merrick Boulevard and pulled up in front of a small crowd of people. It seemed as if everybody and their mother was watching them.

"Check it right, I gotta take care of something real quick but I'll be right back. Y'all got money on y'all?" Eddie asked looking from Mike to Teddy.

"I got a couple of dollars, why—what's up?" Teddy asked, trying to figure out his brother's agenda.

"I got money too nigga! You need to hold something?" Mike interjected as if he had a million dollars.

"Nah, I was just gonna tell y'all to get a couple of bottles of Alize'. I'm gonna get us some bomb ass smoke."

"Okay nigga!" Mike sang, stroking Eddie's ego. "Go 'head and take care of your business and we'll run into the liquor store. After that I'm tryna stop by the Chinese restaurant cause I'm hungry as shit. Cool?"

Teddy had the back door to the Benz open and no sooner than he stepped out, he heard someone call his name.

"Teddy!"

He looked around and saw his man Stan with a gang of niggas around him. Teddy and Stan went to Junior High School together at I.S. 8.

"Big Stan, what's good?" Teddy said with plenty of bass in his voice. He looked around and saw some cuties present and he was happy that his moms had gave him that money for some new Timberlands. Teddy had on some crisp construction Timbs, blue Sean John jeans, a beige Sean John hoodie, and a fitted Yankee cap pulled low.

While Eddie and Mike jumped out the car, Teddy approached Stan and gave him some dap.

"My nigga! It's all about you and the things you do!" Stan commented, staring at the CLS with admiration.

Meanwhile, Eddie was stunting! He left the windows open and the system bumping.

'Cough up a lung, where you from, Marcy son... ain't nothing nice'

Jay-Z's voice momentarily captivated those in the vicinity. The audio was so crisp it was as if Jay was spitting the lyrics live.

'I'm from where the hammers rung, news cameras never come, you and your man hung in every verse of your rhymes...'

Mike went inside the liquor store to cop the Alize' while Eddie went to take care of his business. Teddy remained outside bustin' it up with Stan, and soaking up all the attention he was getting from a few of the homies. Baby boy was feeling like a boss!

"Ayo! I gotta run in here to get me something to eat," he told Stan after his stomach growled for the third time.

"Yeah, yeah! I'll be right here," Stan replied.

Teddy knew that nine times out of ten, Stan was out there selling drugs. Everybody had to eat is the way he saw it.

He went inside the Chinese restaurant and ordered a half a chicken with French fries.

Mike came into the restaurant and, true to form, he started his shit. Teddy wanted to act like he didn't know his crazy ass because a couple of homies came in too.

"Bruce Lee!" Mike yelled, imitating Chris Tucker again. "Give me an order of chicken wings and some beef fried rice, and don't be putting no cats and dogs in my food. I'm watching you!"

The girls in the restaurant fell out laughing! In Chinese, Bruce Lee told his wife: "*Make sure you give this stupid mother fucker a special!*" To Mike, he said, "Chicken wings, beef fried rice, 3.25! You pay now!"

$$$

Teddy was so hungry, he ate all his food and half of Mike's beef fried rice. Mike was cool, he was used to special food, but it didn't take long for Teddy's stomach to start acting up from the special Beef fried rice. He was in the back seat of the Benz balled up and sweating. Eddie looked at his brother through the rear-view mirror as he drove.

"What's wrong witchu, Teddy?" Eddie asked with concern.

"That food fucked by stomach up, I think I gotta take a shit," Teddy said, taking off his fitted hat and setting it on the seat next to him.

"Them Chinese muthafuckas may have pissed in that beef fried rice. You know I was up in there fuckin' with their nasty asses," Mike said nonchalantly.

"I'm gonna drop you off at the house so you can use the bathroom and get yourself together."

They watched as he sprinted into the house as if he was scared that he might shit on himself. Inside, he didn't make any detours; he beelined straight to the bathroom.

Above the sink in the bathroom was a mirror. Above the mirror was the light switch, which Teddy turned on by pulling a silver chain that hung on the side. When Teddy looked into the mirror, he let out a vicious squeal. The kid was almost frightened to death, and that would have been the easy way out. Standing behind Teddy, in his own apartment, was none other than Reggie Ransom!

Reggie gripped the back of Teddy's head and smashed his face against the mirror. A burst of blood spurted over the mirror and splattered onto the porcelain sink. With a big paw, Reggie Ransom cupped Teddy's mouth to stifle his screams.

"Listen to me, Teddy," Reggie Ransom said calmly. "Do you know who I am?"

Teddy knew that this was the man they called the Grim Reaper, but he still shook his head.

"They call me One Shot, Teddy. Do you know why they call me One Shot?"

Again, Teddy shook his head.

"They call me One Shot because that's all you get. I don't have a whole lot of patience, young buck, so I give the people one shot. That's the situation here, Teddy. I'm gonna ask you a question, and I'm only gonna ask you once. Fair enough?"

Teddy was scared! He didn't know what else to do so he nodded his head.

Reggie Ransom gave him a few seconds to get himself together and then he put it out there.

"What – or better yet, *who* – is the star in the mirror?"

Teddy's eyes gaped open.

"This is your one shot," Reggie Ransom reminded him. He removed his hand from Teddy's mouth.

"I, I, I don't..."

Teddy heard a click. In a flash, Reggie Ransom sliced Teddy's throat with a switch blade.

One Shot gripped Teddy's sweatshirt and allowed him to fall to the floor softly. Then, taking his time, he sat on the cold floor and placed Teddy's head in his lap. The scent of feces permeated the heavy air. With a large sewing needle and black thread, Reggie Ransom began to sew Teddy's mouth shut, while at the same time humming an old tune. Blood spilled onto Reggie Ransom's clothes and soaked through to his legs, but he seemed not to notice. When he was done playing doctor, he took a sticky mouse trap and slapped it on Teddy's chest!

CHAPTER SIX

Never trust a big butt and a smile! That was a hot hook in the 90's when Bell Biv Divoe came out with the song *Poison* but in the new millennium Infra-red, Wild Blood, and Makavelli wasn't trying to hear that. They were aboard Yacht Attessa, and it felt as if they had died and gone to heaven. Chicks with phat asses surrounded them and they were smiling like a muthafucka.

The three level, 260-foot Yacht hosted over one hundred select guest whom had attended Del Gibson's wedding.

On the third level, a huge swimming pool was infested with Dons and Divas looking for a way to cool off. Infra-red and Makavelli were staying out of the water but that didn't stop them from throwing women in the pool. When the other women saw them coming, they would either hold their noses and jump in the water voluntarily, or they would haul ass.

Fat Joe's voice was banging throughout the Yacht, and he had all them rocking away and leaning back.

'*I said my niggas don't dance we just pull up our pants and ... do the rock away, and ... lean back ... lean back.*'

The reception was out of control. They were anchored off the coast of Miami, Florida on a beautiful day. A few people ventured off on jet skis while others sat on the ass end of the Attessa with their feet in the water.

On the second level, in a dining and living room setting, Chandar was shaking up a bottle of Cristal. As Del Gibson stood near Jeff White in deep conversation, Chandar expertly popped the cork and began spraying Del Gibson with champagne.

"Oh! Oh shit!" Del Gibson exclaimed, fleeing from the line of fire. "Oh yeah? You doing it like that?"

Del Gibson, A.K.A Dr. Hyde, was drenched!

"Congratulations, Playboy!" Chandar yelled as everybody stood around laughing.

"Where's Erika? We have to get Erika too!" Someone screamed out.

"Y'all better not get me. I just changed my clothes," Erika pleaded from across the room.

Dr. Hyde already had his hands on a bottle of Cris' and he launched an attack on everybody in his path. It was an all-out champagne war! The women were screaming in excitement while the men strategically tried to make their way to the bar that Dr. Hyde was attempting to defend.

Chandar came up behind the C.E.O. of Loud Mouth Records and grabbed him in a bear hug. While they tossed each other around and struggled, Jeff White and a few of the fellas armed themselves with several bottles of champagne. They proceeded to let Dr. Hyde have it, and Chandar was getting drenched too because he was holding him, but he didn't care. He was all for the fun.

Afterward, while Del stood in the middle of the floor soaking wet with the jackass look on his face, his new wife Erika came over and poured another bottle of champagne over his head. Dr. Hyde had a temper that was out of this world and he was about to lose it, but his wife's participation was enough to simmer his anger. He grabbed Erika and pulled her into his chest. He kissed her deeply and everyone in the room began applauding! Chandar whistled loudly while everyone else clapped.

Indeed, this was to be a day to remember. The staff cleaned as best as they could while the guest who were able excused themselves to change clothes. The yacht boasted six bedrooms, and a swimming pool, so those who were smart made sure to bring swimwear and a change of clothes.

The Captain of the ship called for everyone's attention as the sun began to decline in the West. Most of the guests made their way to the second level and crowded into the spacious quarters to see what was going on.

Chandar and his squad posted up by a Baby grand piano as everyone attempted to get settled in.

"It's some bad bitches up in this mafucker here!" Infra-red declared looking around the room.

It was basically standing room only. The staff was coming around with silver platters that held shrimp, Buffalo wings with blue cheese, and goblets of champagne.

A drop dead gorgeous shorty that looked like she was from Brazil was sitting on one of the couches shooting mean looks in Chandar's direction.

"Fuck is wrong with Mommy on the couch?" Chandar asked confused.

Jeff White laughed. "It look like shawty skrate ready to kill somebody," he said in a deep southern accent, straight out of Georgia.

"Ohhh, that's the bitch Makavelli threw in the pool. Ole' girl was acting like she was all that, like her pretty ass wasn't going in the water," Infra-red explained.

The whole squad was looking at shorty now. She rolled her eyes at them and they started laughing.

The Captain took a silver spoon and began to tap it against a Champagne glass to get everyone's attention. When he was satisfied with the silence, he began to speak.

"Ladies and gentlemen...please allow me to formally introduce myself. My name is Donovan. And it brings me great pleasure to be able to cater to all of you, courtesy of Mr. and Mrs. Delmar and Erica Gibson. My staff is coming around with enough champagne for everyone, and I would like to be the first one to make a toast."

As if on cue, one of the staff filled the Captain's empty glass with champagne. After everyone was given a glass, the Captain raised his glass in the air and directed his words towards Dr. Hyde and his new wife.

"To Del and Erica... May the vows that you took today be etched into your hearts, and may you live happily ever after until death do you part."

Someone yelled out 'Amen', and everyone took a sip from their glass.

Next, a little cutie with a nice shape stepped up.

"I wanna make a toast," she began. Her name was Ronnie and she was one of Erika's best friends. "Oh my goodness! Erica, you've been my friend for, like, forever. And I can't lie, Del has really made you happy. Whenever he's around I see a side of you that I haven't seen since we were kids. When you two are together I can honestly see that you be happy, so...congratulations!"

Everyone put their glasses up in the air and took a sip of bubbly.

"Here we go!" Chandar said raising his glass back in the air. "Erika, from a Don to a Diva... you must be a truly amazing woman to be able to make a playa settle down."

"She put his ass in retirement!" Someone interjected, and everyone roared in laughter.

"Exactly!" Chandar agreed. He continued, "I just want to be the one to tell you, you have a good a man in your corner!"

Chandar turned his attention to Del.

"Dr. Hyde...from a boss to a boss! Listen to me... this is black star power at its best. You have a strong woman, not behind you, but right beside you. In order for a marriage to remain strong it's going to take a lot of work... I wish you both the very best. Congratulations!"

The staff were walking around making sure the guest kept a flow of champagne in their glasses. By the time most of the people made a toast, it was dark outside and everyone was good and drunk.

One of Dr. Hyde's homies rocked the crowd by doing a rendition of one of Jagged Edge's songs. He had everyone singing:

"Meet me at the alter in your white dress, we ain't getting no younger we might as well do it..."

While everyone was caught up in the moment, Chandar snuck downstairs with *mami* that Makavelli threw in the pool.

"Why y'all was laughing at me earlier?" She pouted while Chandar led her to one of the rooms that Dr. Hyde let him and his squad use.

"Because your little sexy ass was sitting on that couch like you was mad at the world," Chandar joked as they reached the door to the room.

When he opened the door, Jeff White was sitting in a chair watching two chicks freaking off on the bed.

"Hey Pimpin'! Come in and close the door." He said this as if Chandar and little *mami* were right on time.

"Nah, three is company, Playboy!" Chandar said backing out of the room.

The Big Homie led mami further down the corridor and checked another room. He found it empty. He took the **Do Not Disturb** sign and hung it on the door knob.

$$$

Speed boats pulled up beside the Yacht Attessa throughout the evening as people both came and left the reception.

Infra-red, Wild Blood, and Makavelli were on the third level by the pool, smoking that purple haze when Dr. Hyde came looking for Chandar. The Big Homie and Jeff White had disappeared over an hour ago. Infra-red thought Chandar went to use the bathroom or something. The beautiful women in the pool gave Infra-red's mind something else to focus on, so he wasn't that concerned with where everyone was at.

"I don't know where that fool went, Homie, but I know one thing, he missing a good show," Infra-red said, exhaling the haze as he spoke.

"Send somebody to find him and y'all meet me on the second level in a half an hour. We got business to take care of," Dr. Hyde said, grabbing Infra-red's blunt and taking a few hits before passing it back.

"No doubt, Homie. It's business before pleasure!" Infra-red responded as he got up from the lounge chair he was sitting on. Then to Makavelli and Wild Blood, he said, "Finish up smoking and come down to the second level. I'm going to find Chandar, ya heard?!"

"What's Poppin', fool?"

"Your guess is as good as mine, Homie." Infra-red said as he yawned. It was a long day and niggas was tired. They were ready to snatch some *mamis* up and retire.

By the time Chandar entered the second level quarters with Infra-red and Jeff White, the whole atmosphere had changed. *Careless Whisper* by Wham was playing softly in the background. There were less than twenty people in the room, and a few people were present that Chandar was certain weren't on the Yacht just an hour before. One of those people was Big John, A.K.A. BJ.

BJ was a street nigga that made his way into the music industry and was eating heavily with Irv Gotti and the Murder Inc camp. Chandar ran into BJ often at many of the main events; championship fights, NBA All-Star games, Super bowl weekend, the Kentucky Derby! Whenever the playas played, Chandar ran into BJ. So, while Chandar was making his way over to where his team was, he stopped briefly to acknowledge the player.

"What's good, Playboy?" He said giving BJ dap.

"Oh shit! What up, yo!" BJ responded eagerly. "We be bumping heads everywhere!"

"That's what's up, Player! Niggaz is ballin' on land and sea," Chandar said, giving Big John a manly hug.

"No doubt!" BJ agreed.

Chandar made his way over to where Makavelli and Wild Blood were.

"Where you and that nigga Jeff was at?" Makavelli asked with a smirk.

Jeff White laughed. "Chandar was creeping with shawty you threw in the pool."

"Don't hate the player, hate the game," Chandar joked, sliding in a leather recliner that his team had been holding for him.

"You smashed dat?" Wild Blood asked.

"Nope, I just needed somebody to talk to," Chandar lied with a sly grin.

"And I'm the Pope!" Jeff White cackled. He knew damn well Chandar wasn't doing no talking all that time.

"Anyway, what about y'all? Y'all fools didn't get your freak on?" Chandar asked, looking around at his team.

When niggas remained silent, Chandar shook his head. "That's crazy!" He said it so loud that people looked in their direction. One of the ladies eyeing them looked real familiar.

"What's up with the little cutie with the mole on her face?" Infra-red asked, licking his lips like he was L.L.

"That's Teri," Jeff White informed him. Being the CEO of Colossal Publishing, he knew everybody who was somebody in the literary world.

"Word?" Makavelli said, looking shorty up and down. "I might need to holla at her sexy ass."

"Red light, nigga!" Chandar barked.

"What dawg? I ain't being disrespectful, I'm feeling everything about ole' girl," Makavelli protested.

"I know you ain't being disrespectful, fool, but baby girl is off limits. The Homie Don John be doing business with her kid's father. What's his name Jeff?" Chandar asked looking over his shoulder at his comrade.

"Everybody calls him Lou," Jeff answered. He craned his head over the crowd and nodded toward a tall man. "That's him over there talking to Dr. Hyde."

Chandar's squad was checking dude out when Del Gibson called for everybody's attention. He stepped to the center of the room pulling his wife along.

"I know y'all are wondering why I called this meeting," he said as he smothered Erika with a big hug. "Without a doubt, this is the happiest day of my life!"

Somebody from the crowd cooed, "Awwwwww!"

Dr. Hyde continued, "It may be one of the most difficult, too, because I was faced with a very difficult decision. Those close to me know that I started Loud Mouth Records in an attempt to keep my baby brother out of trouble. The more time and energy I invested in my company, the more I fell in love with it. My baby brother, Deez, he fell in love with it also. However, the company wasn't enough to keep Deez out of trouble. So, now I called all of you here because..." He paused to gauge the temperature of the room. Then, he dropped his bombshell, "I'm selling the label!"

The small crowd was shocked by this revelation, and a buzz went through the room as everyone made comments.

"I handpicked a few people who are in this room, and I'm prepared to allow them to bid for the company, if they desire to do so. My choices are as follows..." He looked at each man as he addressed him.

"Big John, I chose you because of your knowledge of the industry. You've been around a few vets and you know the mechanics and what it takes for a label to succeed, and I know you're ready to pave your own path."

The people around BJ patted him on the back, acknowledging his transition into the game.

Dr. Hyde continued, "My man Lou... I chose you because of your work ethic. You and Teri are selling books like it's crack, and I know you have the dedication and resources to take this label to another level. Besides that, just like BJ, I know you're ready to pave your own path."

Lou nodded his head in agreement, and Teri slid her arm through his in silent support.

"My last choice but definitely not my least, is Chandar! I chose you Big Homie because you actually came highly recommended. Your success with club Arizona's in Brooklyn, your accomplishments in Las Vegas, the innovation you inspired at Colossal Publishing through Jeff White..." Dr. Hyde cast his eyes upward, as if reliving each feat. "It's agreed that everything you touch turns to gold.

"These are my three choices, and these are the people I'd feel comfortable with running my company. The bid is starting at five million dollars. Is there anyone here who declines to bid?"

Del Gibson scanned the room. When he was certain that his three choices were ready to bid, he sent his man Vinny Garrett around with blank paper, envelopes, and a synopsis of the company's acquisitions. The three choices were instructed to write their highest bid on the piece of paper they were given and place the paper inside the envelopes.

BJ and his associates were in deep conversation, as were Lou and Teri. Chandar didn't confide in anyone. After bringing him the synopsis, he just wrote his bid on the piece of paper and placed it inside the envelope.

When Del Gibson was in possession of the three envelopes, he examined the contents of each before he announced that there was a new CEO of Loud Mouth Records.

"My friends and invited guest, I announce to you the new owner and CEO of Loud Mouth Records..." All eyes were on him as the room waited on his announcement with abated breath. "Without further ado, give our congratulations to... Mr. Chandar Grant!"

Everyone in the room applauded the ghetto star. People came over and shook his hand and patted his back. BJ was the only one candid enough to ask the million-dollar question.

"What was your bid?"

Chandar brushed him off politely, but firmly. "That ain't about nothing, playboy. It's over."

When Lou and Teri came over, the smiles appeared to be genuine. They both wished Chandar the best.

"Thank you!" Chandar gushed with a genuine smile. "Y'all just make sure y'all do good by my fam, Don John. Give him what his hands call for. That fool is bringing loyalty to the table that just don't exist no more, I suggest y'all make him feel at home."

This wasn't a threat; Chandar was offering sincere advice.

"No doubt! That's my Homie," Lou assured him.

Lou and Don John were from the same neighborhood. This is why Chandar forbade the wolves from being disrespectful and trying to holla at Lou's girl.

Chandar gave Lou dap and a brotherly hug, then he embraced Teri and whished her the best in her endeavors.

When Chandar turned around, Dr. Hyde was standing there smiling.

"You think you're slick, don't you?" Dr. Hyde asked. He was holding the three envelopes in his hand.

"Obviously slicker than your other two choices," Chandar shot back. "How much did I get it for?"

"Eleven million." Dr. Hyde held out the bids for Chandar to see.

BJ had bid 8.5 million. Lou bid 10 million. On Chandar's piece of paper, he wrote: *The highest bid, plus ten percent.*

Genius.

CHAPTER SEVEN

Jerry Moore was sitting in his wheelchair in front of his cell, reading a Don Diva magazine. There was no doubt in his mind that this publication was indeed the street Bible.

Jerry Moore was reflecting on the words of Kevin Chiles, the Publisher of the magazine, who was relaying a very important lesson he learned from his beloved mother— *'Nobody likes a tattle tale.'* This was translated to mean: **Nobody likes a snitch!**

The message that Jerry Moore received from that particular issue of Don Diva was that all snitches appeared to be someone other than whom they actually were, until a situation occurred that forced them to reveal their true identity. In other words, most snitches appeared to be the ride or die, bout-it bout-it, down for whatever type of dudes, when in fact they were cowards hiding behind their masks.

This is what Jerry Moore was thinking when he spotted Mr. Swab, the unit counselor, walking toward his office. Spinning his wheelchair around with a skill he developed over a period of time, the Big Homie sought to catch the counselor before the *hot* dudes bombarded the office.

"Ayo Swab!" He hollered as the counselor put his key in the office door.

Mr. Swab turned around at the same time he twisted the door knob and pushed the office door open.

"Ayo Moore!" He responded as Jerry Moore approached him.

"What, you mocking me?"

"No, no, Mr. Moore, I'm just messing with you. What do you need?" The counselor asked, walking into his office.

Jerry Moore followed him into the office. Inside, a huge wooden desk was crammed into the small office. There was a stack of paperwork on the desk next to a coffee cup and half-eaten donut. A stapler laid on its side next to a calendar and organizer. Pictures of who Jerry Moore assumed was Mr. Swab's family were situated behind the telephone that was ringing incessantly.

"Hello?" Mr. Swab snapped after placing the phone to his ear.

"No, this is Mr. Swab on I-63," he said into the receiver. "Try extension 4169."

When Mr. Swab hung the phone up, one of the unit orderlies came barging into his office.

"Mr. Swab, you gonna let me get that phone call today?" He pleaded as if he'd been waiting for a phone call forever.

"Nigga, do I come barging in this office when you're in here trying to take care of bizness???" Jerry Moore barked, looking at dude as if he was crazy. Jerry Moore might have been in a wheelchair, but his name stood tall.

"Oh, excuse me. I didn't know, I was just—I'll come back later." The guy stammered as he backed out of the office.

"I need to have you around more often," Mr. Swab joked in seriousness. "It be hectic around here. I try to do a little of everything but never seem to get anything done."

"That's because you be having these *hot* dudes up in here brown-nosing all the time."

Mr. Swab chuckled, "You wouldn't understand. I have to cover my ass just like you guys. If I don't, the snitches will tell on my black ass too. So, I tolerate them. But, believe you me, nobody likes a snitch, not even the government."

This statement caused Jerry Moore to smile. "You know what, Swab? Somebody told me that you was a good dude. That's what's up! You do what you gotta do to keep your job and don't let these hot ass dudes trap you off. I'm just trying to make a phone call and I'm out your way. You think that's possible?"

Mr. Swab looked at the Big Homie in admiration. Jerry Moore didn't know that Mr. Swab had grown up in Brownsville, in the same neighborhood where Jerry Moore and Chandar were hood legends. The counselor didn't intend to reveal this, but he planned on doing everything in his power to make sure the ghetto star wanted for nothing throughout his stay on I-63.

Mr. Swab picked up the phone, punched nine to get an outside line, and said to Jerry Moore, "What's the number?"

$$$

Later that night, when Jerry Moore and Barkim were locked in their cell for the night, the Big Homie had a lot to talk about.

The counselor, Swab, had allowed Jerry Moore to call Chandar on an unmonitored phone, and let them stay on the phone for almost an hour.

Then at mail call, Jerry Moore got three pieces of mail. A letter from his mom, and two letters from his main chick, LaShawn. The letter from his mom was short and to the point. She reminded him that she loved him and that she was there for him, no matter what. LaShawn's letters, however, was hot and steamy, the kind that created a need to take a cold shower. She even included some sexy pictures of her and one of her girlfriends wearing thongs to provide the visuals. Yeah, that was definitely that work, and Jerry Moore was grateful.

Barkim was at the small desk hooking up some tuna fish for them to eat on crackers while Jerry Moore talked about the day's events and did some reminiscing.

"That nigga Chandar is down in Miami chillin', son! He was at Del Gibson's wedding. Remember I was telling you that I was the A&R over at Loud Mouth Records?"

Barkim squeezed mayonnaise into the tuna fish. "Yeah, I remember the mixtape y'all put out with G-Bundles and Bugsy—that joint was fire!"

"Okay listen to this, you ain't gonna believe this, son. That nigga Chandar just bought Loud Mouth Records!"

"Get the fuck outta here, Homie. That's what's up!" Barkim said. He nodded his head while mixing the tuna.

"Damn, son! We're stuck in this sucka ass shit and niggaz is out there doing it up."

"Don't even sweat that, Homie. We'll be there in a minute," Barkim replied with optimism.

Jerry Moore cut his eyes at Barkim and shook his head. Everybody in jail said that same shit! You ask a dude in jail when he coming home, and nine times out of ten, he'll say, 'I'll be there in a minute.' Even dudes with *elbows* (Life sentences) be screaming the same shit. Let them tell it, a minute is a long ass time.

Barkim scooped out a spoon of tuna and held it out for a taste test. Jerry Moore stuck his hand out and Barkim dumped the tuna in his hand. The Big Homie threw it in his mouth and after two seconds he said, "Unh huh! All that need is a hit of honey to take it over the top. Where the crackers at?"

Barkim added some honey to the tuna and pulled out a sleeve of Town House crackers. A minute later and they were in the cell getting their eat on.

"You hear me, Bar?" Jerry Moore asked with a mouth full of food. "I love that nigga, Chandar! I remember when we first met, we were in Special ED, together, ya heard?!?" Jerry Moore plastered a big smile on his face as he remembered his first encounter with Chandar.

"Y'all was in the same class?"

"Yeah, yeah. I whipped that nigga Chandar's ass when we first met. I was fucking with him about his name calling him Chandelier. He started getting mad and shit, so I told the nigga, 'I don't give a fuck if you get mad!' And then this nigga started acting like he wanted to fight. So, you know I whipped that ass. He fought back though, he was the only one who wasn't scared to fight me. I guess that's why we ended up getting so close."

"It's your story, Homie, you can tell it any way you wanna tell it," Barkim said, laughing as if he didn't believe Jerry Moore had actually beaten Chandar. "If that was me, we would've been fighting every day."

"Yeah, and you would've got your ass whooped every day!" Jerry Moore promised him, nodding his head up and down. "I probably wouldn't have even fought you, Bar! You probably would've been the O.G. in our crew, you might've been able to stop us from making some of the mistakes we made."

"Homie, you and your boy accomplished what others may never accomplish in a lifetime. When y'all die, the hood will still be talking about the things y'all did, so don't talk to me about mistakes. I'm ten years your senior, Homie, and let me tell you something, I look up to you and Chandar. I have nothing but respect for y'all."

Jerry Moore smiled, but the excitement that was in the room just a minute ago was gone. Regardless of what Barkim thought, the Big Homie knew that they indeed made mistakes. One of their mistakes was the reason Jerry Moore was now confined to a wheelchair.

"That's what's up! I respect you too Homie, but you're wrong if you believe that me and Chandar didn't make mistakes. You hear me, fool? Do you know who did this to my legs?" The Big Homie asked, his tone becoming deadly.

"A Crip?" Barkim asked, because he really wasn't sure. This was a topic Jerry Moore never talked about.

The Big Homie peeled off his white tee and ran his fingers over the two scars that tarnished his chest.

"Yeah, he was a Crip alright, but this nigga wasn't a gangbanger. I think he just used that Crip shit to camouflage who he really was. This niggaz family was a gang, he had no reason to be affiliated. With the last name, Cook, that nigga had everything he wanted without being gang related."

"You mean to tell me somebody in the Cook family did that to you?" Barkim asked in amazement.

Jerry Moore nodded. His eyes glazed over with malice as he relived the memory.

"Kevin Cook, Big Willie's nephew. I punished that nigga almost ten years ago, but I made the mistake of leaving him alive. I actually tried to kill his ass, but Chandar pulled me off of him because Lisa was screaming and crying and shit. This is before Lisa became Chandar's baby's mother."

"That's the one that William Cook's people killed at the train yards, right?"

Jerry Moore nodded again. "That was a mistake that cost William Cook his life. Chandar and the Homie went super hard on that fool after that, they ran up in the funeral parlor and the whole nine. That shit was crazy!"

Barkim was extremely quiet as Jerry Moore revealed the wholesale death that his Homies dealt to the William Cook Organization. Barkim had heard the rumors, but this was the first time that all the stories were confirmed.

Jerry Moore was slippin'! He knew from '*Peep Game 101*' that *loose lips sink ships,* yet there he was, bumping his gums together like he swallowed a radio. Hopefully his words wouldn't come back to haunt him, but the Big Homie should've learned a lesson from the Don Diva Magazine he'd read earlier that day.

'**All snitches appear to be someone other than whom they actually are...until a situation occurs that forces them to reveal their true colors.**'

Barkim may have been remembered as a standup dude, but 24 hours a day, 7 days a week, the rule remained the same: **Trust No One!!**

CHAPTER EIGHT

The gold CLS 500 Mercedes Benz floated down Guy R. Brewer Blvd. Big Time felt like the ultimate gangsta as he maneuvered his V through the 'hood. A survivor of the Jerry Moore era, Big Time understood the fact that anybody could be touched! Still, now that the storm was over, it was hard not to feel as if he was invincible. He made it through the storm! The truth was that Big Time had come up. He wasn't smart enough to purchase a home yet, but he had a brand-new Benz, a Cadillac Escalade, and he was renting a nice three-bedroom apartment around the way. No one advised him to invest his money, so all his savings went inside a safe that he kept in his bedroom closet. It was these things, along with a new connect, that made Big Time feel as if he was above the law.

As he drove past Baisley Projects, he put on his signal to make a left turn on 116th Avenue. He banged a few more corners, getting deep in the back streets, until he pulled up in front of a group of people on 115th Ave and 155th Street. Big Time pushed a button and the passenger side window glided down.

"Ayo Booga! Where Kool-Aid?" Big Time yelled to one of the guys posted up on the corner.

"He just went in the house, you want me to get 'im?

"Yeah, and tell him I said bring that with him."

While Booga ran to get Kool-Aid, the other guys that were standing on the corner greeted Big Time. One dude named Trey came over to the car.

"Big Time, what's good?"

"That paper, Trey! I'm chasing that."

"I see! When you gonna let me roll with you and get some real money?" The young solider asked.

Everybody was waiting for their shot at touching major paper, but Big Time knew that most people wanted something handed to them. Nobody wanted to work their way up.

"What you bringing to the table, Trey? If you roll with me, you gonna have to put that work in! It cost to floss."

"I'm ready to do whatever you need me to do, I ain't scared of no work!" Trey said sounding sincere.

"I'll get back with you," Big Time said as Kool-Aid slid into the passenger seat.

"Alright, bet." Trey said.

Big Time checked the mirror before pulling off.

"Kool-Aid, what's up?" Big Time said looking over at his Homie.

Kool-Aid had a Gap bag in his lap that appeared to be bursting at the seams.

"Everything is everything! I got ten grand for you right here," Kool-Aid responded as he played with the CD changer. He found the *'Get Rich Or Die Trying'* CD and put on one of his favorite songs. The music blared from the speakers with clarity and Kool-Aid nodded his head up and down.

'It's 50 A.K.A. Ferarri F50.... See you a wanksta and you need to stop frontin'...'

Kool-Aid looked at Big Time and reflected on what the streets were saying. The word was that when Jerry Moore was on the loose, Big Time couldn't eat. If this was true, that might qualify Big Time as a wanksta.

'Say you a gangsta but you never popped nothing....'

Kool-Aid recalled on more than one occasion while Jerry Moore was home that Big Time said he was going over to Baisley to talk to the Big Homie. He may have been sincere, but he definitely never got around to doing it.

Then the nigga Peanut started snitching and Jerry Moore got locked up. Not long after that, Reggie Ransom approached Kool-Aid and gave him an ultimatum: kill Peanut, or risk having his whole squad annihilated.

'You ain't no friend of mine, you ain't no kin of mine, what makes you think that I won't run up on you with the nine...'

As 50 chanted in the background, Kool-Aid continued to reminisce.

Kool-Aid was a cold soldier and a stand-up dude who respected the code of the streets. He assured Reggie Ransom the problem would be dealt with. Kool-Aid didn't confide in anyone, not even Big Time. He just did what needed to be done. Their hustle was going too good to allow a snitch ass nigga to jeopardize it.

Big Time pulled his car up in front of a house on 112th Avenue. Mike and a dark-skinned chick were standing on the steps of the house. Big Time got out the car and came around to meet Mike.

"There that nigga go right there! What's really good, hustler?" Mike said giving Big Time dap.

"Just trying to keep my head above the water," Big Time said, scanning the block. "What's good around here?"

"I can't even lie, it's been jive slow since Teddy got killed. The po-leece around here like they still tryna catch O.J. and shit," Mike said in his Chris Tucker voice.

Big Time's expression saddened. "They still don't know who did it?" He asked.

"Shiiit, all fingers are pointing at the Grim Reaper." Mike said this like it was obvious.

"Reggie Ransom, huh?"

"Yerp!" Mike confirmed. "I got some money for you, you came to pick up?"

"Yeah, where Eddie at?"

"He left some money for you, too, but you know he's taking it kinda bad. That was his twin, man."

"Yeah, that's fucked up what happened," Big Time agreed. "How much money you got all together?"

"Almost eight grand."

"Damn!"

"What? I got a little something in the stash if you need it."

"Yeah, I needed ten. I'm tryna make a move."

"Wait right here!" Mike said, and ran into the house.

The dark-skinned girl on the steps kept licking her lips and stealing glances at Big Time the entire time he and Mike were discussing business.

"Your little sexy ass don't gotta sneak and peak, Ma!" Big Time yelled blowing Shorty spot up. Her smile lit the whole block up.

Mike came out the house with a brown paper bag that held the money in it.

"I'm poppin', you don't gotta count it, it's all there money!" Mike sang as he passed Big Time the bag.

"That's what I like to hear." Big Time nodded his head vigorously. "Listen, what's up with chocolate right there, that's you?" Big Time asked loud enough for shorty to hear.

"Nah, that's my homegirl, Dee. You tryna holla?"

"Hell yeah," Big Time said as he went around the car. "Give ole' girl my cell number."

Big Time plopped back in the car and blasted 50 Cent's 'In Da Club' as he pulled off.

'Go, go, go Shawty, it's your birthday! We gonna party like it's your birthday...'

They were on a dead-end block so Big Time had to make a U-turn to exit. When he drove past Mike, Chocolate was waving bye flashing all thirty-two so bright it nearly blinded him. Big Time tapped the horn twice and kept it moving.

Minutes Later...

Stan and his squad were posted up on Merrick Boulevard getting their grind on when the gold Benz pulled up to the curb. The last time Teddy was seen alive, he was in that car.

Double parking in front of the Chinese restaurant, Big Time jumped out the whip and approached the group.

"Stan the man, what's good?" He asked giving a few of the guys dap.

"Money over bitches, son! Who's car is that?" Stan asked, attempting to sound as nonchalant as possible.

"That's me, why? You don't like it?"

"Nah, I was just wondering because my little man Teddy was in that same car before he got killed."

"Oh....yeah," Big Time said, softening his tone. "We tryin' to find out what happened now. That was my peoples, I let his twin get his floss on and they was together before that shit happened."

"If you find out who did that, holla at me and we can take care of that together," Stan said frontin' He didn't even fuck with Teddy like that.

"No doubt," Big Time promised, frontin' right along with him. None of them niggaz was going to do a damn thing about Teddy getting killed.

"Who's upstairs?" Big Time asked, getting down to business.

"Trigger. We got about fifteen up there for you, but we probably gonna need some more stuff before the night is over."

"I got you," Big Time said as he went to get that money.

They actually only had twelve grand for him, but that was cool because Big Time only was looking for ten. He gave Kool-Aid three grand and he put four in his pocket. He owed his connect twenty-five. They gathered the stacks and put the twenty-five grand in the Gap bag that Kool-Aid brought. Minutes later, Big Time was flashing out on the Grand Central Expressway.

Big Time drove to the Hoyt Avenue exit. He had called his connect and they agreed to meet at a small diner a few blocks away from the Waldorf Astoria.

After instructing Kool-Aid to stay put in the car, Big Time entered the diner with Gap bag in hand. He spotted his connect sitting in a booth near the back. Big Time slid in the booth across from him and put the Gap bag on the table, pushing it toward the connect.

"Twenty-five grand, Big Dawg."

The connect, a black guy in his late twenties, pushed the Gap bag right back in Big Time's direction. He glanced around casually, then placed a black briefcase on the table. He slid it over to Big Time.

"I thought we understood each other concerning paper and plastic bags? I can't walk out of here with that," The connect said as if the Gap bag was a pile of shit.

"You right, that's my bad. I was rushin', I didn't have time to grab anything else."

"Well try not to let it happen again. It's sloppy, and we don't have room for mistakes."

"You right, I'm wrong," Big Time acknowledged for the second time.

His connect studied his facial expression and body language to see if he was being sarcastic or rebellious. After concluding it was neither, he spoke again, "Put the money in the briefcase and take the contents out of the briefcase and put it inside of your plastic bag."

Big Time looked around before dumping the money on the seat beside him. There were twenty-five stacks of thousand-dollar bundles held together by rubber bands. Next, he opened the briefcase. Two kilos of pretty cocaine smiled at him. He fought the urge to smile right back at them as he removed them from the briefcase and placed them in the Gap bag. He quickly loaded the briefcase with the money and closed it up before sliding it across the table.

With that out of the way, the connect began to relax. He took a sip of coffee and began to question Big Time about some of the things going on in the hood.

"What are the streets saying about the murder of your new associate?"

"Who Teddy?" Big Time asked.

The connect nodded his head up and down. Big Time took a deep breath and exhaled slowly.

"The dude Reggie Ransom' name keep coming up. A girl named Robin said she saw him creeping around the house before it happened."

"Robin? What's her last name?" The connect asked.

"I don't know her last name?"

"Find out! We need to put Mr. Ransom's lights out."

"I'll find out what I can."

"I need this information like yesterday, Big Time. If what the streets are saying is true, this is the same guy who offed Peanut."

Big Time leaned in. "They say he's been asking about the Star in the Mirror," he whispered.

The connect's eyebrows arched. He studied Big Times's facial expression carefully. This time, Big Time didn't distort his facial expression. In this instance, Big Time didn't avert his gaze. This time, he and the connect stared at each other until the connect finally spoke again.

"That's because somebody is talking too much, and loose lips sink ships," he surmised.

"Hurry up and get me that information on Reggie Ransom. He's barking up the wrong fucking tree now! The star in the mirror is shining."

CHAPTER NINE

They say a picture expresses a thousand words. This is the maxim that came to mind as Chandar and his guest stared at the life size portrait that hung above the fire place. It was a portrait of three boys, each about eight years old. The picture was taken in a public housing project. Broken glass everywhere, empty beer cans, and other kids in the background, oblivious to the fact that a piece of history was being preserved. In the picture, three kids posed as if they were young gangstas.

The boy in the middle was clutching a brown paper bag, probably filled with candy, and his hat was tilted to the side. He looked into the camera with a seriousness unbecoming of a boy his age. His demeanor screamed: *I'm the leader, and I know it!*

The boy to his left had his arms folded across his chest in a gesture of authority, while the boy on the right stood with his hands on his hips, and a menacing scowl on his face.

This was a memory of Chandar as a youth, captured and frozen.

"Look at the look on Shorty face that got his hands on his hips," Jerome Smith said pointing at the picture.

"I believe his little ass was reincarnated," Jeff White said. "It look like he been here before."

"Chandar the one that kill me. Even when he was little he was holding the bag. My baby was destined to be a boss!" Karen said, leaning her head on Chandar's shoulder.

They were in the family room of Chandar and Karen's home out on Long Island.

Chandar had invited Jerome Smith, who was the leader of the 121st Street Crips, to their home to talk about new ways to strengthen the movement called C.A.B.B.A.G.E. The acronym stood for, Crips and Bloods Banging Against Gang Enmity. The movement was successful thus far, and was responsible for bringing Crips and Bloods together for basketball tournaments, group trips, and block parties among other things.

Jeff White was at the house to discuss the deal with Loud Mouth Records. Truthfully, Chandar didn't have eleven million dollars at his disposal that he could just throw into one venture. Also with his shady past, he didn't want to chance being thrust into the limelight on the East Coast, especially at a time when Jerry Moore was a regular in the daily newspapers. For this reason, Jeff White would be a better choice to be the owner of Loud Mouth Records...at least on paper.

Chandar reached over and rubbed Karen's protruding stomach. "It takes a boss to know a boss," he said, before kissing her on the forehead. He turned his attention to Jerome Smith. "Jerome, let me ask you a question. What do you think we can do to take the Cabbage Movement to another level?"

Jerome walked away from the portrait he'd been admiring and sat back down on the sofa. He clasped his chin in his hand, pondering the question. When he spoke, his words were measured.

"For real, for real...I think we doing a good job. The only thing I think we should do is expand, get other neighborhoods involved. Eventually we can unite the Crips and Bloods on the whole' East Coast. After that, we can start heading West."

They both knew this was easier said than done.

"For now, let's look at Brooklyn and Queens," Chandar suggested. "I can basically get with the O.G.'s, all the Blood sets that fall under United Bloods in Tune – UBN. I can show them what we were able to do and initiate peace talks. Once I demonstrate that this move will be beneficial to all who participate, I think I can sway the Bloods. The question is, are you in a position to do the same thing with the Crips?"

Jerome's face twisted into a mask of uncertainty. "That, I can honestly say I don't know. There's way more Crip sets than there are Blood – "

"You can't be serious," Chandar interjected.

"You know why I say that? Because Crips be on the low, niggaz be Crippin' and you won't even know because our rules allow us to conceal it. But, no doubt, I'll definitely give it a shot. I'm just saying, my job might be a little harder."

"Nothing worth having comes easy, Playboy." Chandar said dismissively, and then softened the lesson with, "If I can help you with anything, just holla."

Karen lifted her head up from Chandar's shoulder so he could get up and escort his company to the door.

At the door Chandar gave Jerome dap and patted him on the back. "Get as many sets as you can involved and we'll get back together to set things in motion," Chandar instructed, giving Jerome his marching orders before he walked out the door.

Chandar picked up the Daily Newspaper off the porch and went back inside the house, paying the newspaper no mind.

In the family room, Karen had disappeared and Jeff White had returned back to admiring the life size portrait of Chandar as a kid.

"Who's the other two boys in the picture with you," Jeff White asked. "Where they is?"

Chandar's expression saddened. "That's Corey D and Mann, they went back to the essence. It's ironic because they was killed almost in the exact location, but it was four years apart."

"Sorry to hear that," Jeff White said respectfully.

"It's been a while," Chandar said. He stared at the portrait for a moment while still holding the newspaper. Then, he took a seat in his favorite chair and got back to business.

"About that deal with Del," Chandar continued as if he hadn't missed a beat. "I was thinking you should play a major part in this deal. I can't afford to be on the front line with this, and you may actually be a better man for the job. So, this is what I propose..." Chandar took a deep breath and came out with it. "You put up five mil, I'll put up four, and I'll get Wild Blood and Infra-red to put up a mil a piece. That way you'll be a majority partner and I can play the background. What you think about that?"

Jeff White was a smooth dude. His deep waves and crisp lineup on his beard announced him as a pretty boy without him even speaking. He crossed his legs and looked as if he was in deep thought. He briefly contemplated the proposal then answered.

"It's up to you, Pimpin'. If that's the way you wanna do it, I got your back. I'm from the street like you, so I understand."

"That's what's up, Playboy," Chandar said with a smile. "Get with your legal team and have them look over the paperwork so we can close this deal."

"It's as good as done," Jeff White promised.

With that out of the way, Chandar began to relax. He opened up the newspaper and couldn't believe what was on the front page. His mouth gaped open while he digested the information in the article:

Batman and Robin Nabbed!

Feds put an end to a network of crooked cops!

Story on page 3

$$$

'It's just one of those days...that a girl goes through, when you're angry inside...'

Monica's song mirrored the way Karen was feeling. Since she reached her final trimester her emotions were jacked off. One minute she'd be laughing and the next she'd be crying. Ole' girl was going through it!

Karen was actually mad at Chandar for leaving her when he went to Miami. Her self-esteem was low, and she thought he was trying to get away from her because she was pregnant. The bigger her stomach grew, the more undesirable she felt.

Then there was the fact that Karen was harboring a secret, one so dark she cringed just thinking about Chandar ever finding out.

A soft knock at her bedroom door startled Karen. She sat up on her bed and attempted to dry her eyes. For a split second, she actually thought Chandar had read her mind and discovered her wicked secret. The thought alone made her cringe.

"Come in," Karen called out softly after getting herself together.

Her girlfriend Jada came into the room and Karen forced a smile.

"Hey girl, what you doing cooped up in this room by yourself?" Jada asked.

"Just thinking," Karen replied, dryly. "I see you finally decided to drop by," she added, popping a stick of Double Mint Gum in her mouth. She offered Jada a piece.

"No thank you, I have my own," Jada said, sitting on the bed. "Chandar said he'll be back in about an hour. Are you guys having problems or something?"

"No, why would you ask that?" Karen asked looking at her friend.

"Because it looks like you was crying," Jada stated firmly.

Karen hated when people were all up in her business, but the truth was, she needed someone to talk to. She knew she could trust Jada but she was unsure if she was ready to confide her problem. She had kept her secret bottled up for almost eight months now.

"No, we're not having problems," Karen whispered, looking far off into the eggshell colored wall.

"You wanna talk about it?" Jada asked, placing her hand on Karen's lap.

"Did I say I wanted to talk about it?" Karen snapped.

'It's just one of those days....don't take it personal...' Monica sang, punctuating their mood.

"Excuse me for wanting to help," Jada said.

"I'm sorry, I didn't mean to bite your head off. This is just...it's a rough time for me."

"That's why I'm here, Karen. That's what friends are for! I was emotional too when I was pregnant with Javon. You have to stay positive."

"I know, Jada, and I'm trying, but I'm in a lot of trouble." Karen said, breaking down and crying again.

Jada put her arms around her friend and tried to console her.

"It's okay, Karen. Go ahead and let it out."

"It's not okay!" Karen sobbed.

"What's not okay, Karen? What is it?"

Karen was crying so hysterically she could barely speak. "Ch...Chandar...he's...he's going to leave me!" She cried.

"That's ridiculous. Why would Chandar leave you?"

"Because ... because I was fucking Kevin."

"Kevin who, Karen?"

"K- Kevin," she stammered. "Kevin Cook."

"You mean Blueberry-Loc?"

Karen nodded.

Jada tried to mask her shock. She had no idea that Karen was creeping with Blueberry-Loc!

"But Karen, Blueberry-Loc is dead. How would Chandar find out you had sex with him? And wait a minute, that had to be before you got involved with Chandar anyway, so I don't understand—"

Karen bawled and bared her truth. "I don't know whose baby is in my stomach!"

CHAPTER TEN

Wisdom is a great teacher! A wise person once proclaimed, *You are who you are today, because of things you chose to do yesterday!*

That being the case, a person who had a hard time staying away from food yesterday, may be having a hard time dealing with obesity today. A person who experimented with drugs yesterday, may be regarded as an addict today.

And a police officer who crossed the line and became a crooked cop yesterday, may be in some deep shit today.

This was the present reality of Batman & Robin. The two corrupt cops were knee deep in a huge pile of shit.

As grave as the matter was, for some reason, the F.B.I. Agents seemed to be in high spirits as they waited for the commissioner, Harry Copeland, to join the meeting. This was to be the second debriefing of John O'Conner and Bill Doherty since the duo were collared over two weeks ago. As they sat waiting for the next phase of their fate, one of the Special Agents was in the middle of a joke.

"So, the man with no arms goes to the roof of a tall building. *This is it!* He thinks as he stands at the edge preparing to leap to his demise. A life with no arms just wasn't a life worth living, was his reasoning.

"But then, as he's standing there contemplating suicide, lo' and behold, he sees another man with no arms down below. The man on the ground is dancing around and he appears to be enjoying life, even without his arms.

"So, the man with no arms who was contemplating suicide runs downstairs at top speed, right?"

The agent's eyes bucked and his arms flailed as he told his joke. In his mind, he was the next Kevin Hart. He continued,

"Somehow he's able to exit the building – don't ask me how; someone must've held the door for him. He runs outside and approaches the other man with no arms. He says, 'man, you just saved my life! I was thinking about throwing myself from the building because of my situation. I can't play baseball like normal people, I can't drive a car, I'll never be arrested for armed robbery – it's depressing! But then, I see you down here dancing around and enjoying life, and you share the same plight as me. I beg you, please share your secret. How do you do it?'

"The other man with no arms was still doing his little dance. He said, 'what are you, some kind of moron or something? It looks like I'm dancing, does it? Well, I'm not you, you imbecile! I'm not dancing, I'm trying to scratch my ass!!!'"

This brought everyone to tears! Everyone in the room doubled over in laughter. Everyone except for Batman & Robin, that is.

John O'Conner had a fake smile on his face, but his partner, Bill Doherty, was fed up and it showed. Bill didn't think that this was a good time for jokes. In fact, being a member of law enforcement for over a decade, he knew that the agents were being facetious with their tardiness. Bill Doherty was two seconds away from exploding when Harry Copeland finally entered the room.

"Gentlemen, I apologize for keeping you waiting," the Commissioner offered casually, as he took a seat.

The Batman & Robin collar was high profile, but many of the agents were still curious about the Commissioner's interest in this particular case. For some reason, he insisted on being involved personally.

"Mr. O'Conner, Mr. Doherty, are you comfortable? Can we get you guys anything before we start?" The Commissioner asked.

"Some coffee would be nice," John O'Conner pointed out. "And are these handcuffs necessary? With all due respect, sir – "

"Clarence, bring the boys some coffee! And someone please remove their cuffs."

The agents shared a puzzled look with each other, but they did as instructed. When everyone was settled in, the meeting began.

"Before we start the recorder, let me just say this..." Harry Copeland began. He cleared his throat and turned his attention to Batman & Robin. "Everyone in this room knows it's impossible to bullshit a bullshitter. Gentlemen, let's not waste any more time with frivolous issues. We got nowhere with the last session and we all know it. Please, no more bullshit? I want to know how you guys came to know Anthony Orena, and I want information that will help us bring him down."

The commissioner gave the signal and one of the agents started the recorder. An uncomfortable silence descended on the room as the agents waited for Batman & Robin to spill the beans.

And then it happened... John O'Conner took a deep breath, exhaled slowly, and then he spoke.

"I first met Anthony Orena in the summer of 1995 at an Italian restaurant in the Sheepshead's Bay section of Brooklyn. I was with Artie – God bless his soul. Artie Mullaney. We were supposed to – "

"Sorry John, when you say Artie are you referring to Arthur Mullaney? The detective who disappeared that same summer?" One of the agents asked.

"That's the one," John O'Conner confirmed, before continuing, "We were supposed to pick up some cash from Olive Oil Carmine from the Gambino family, and there was some type of discrepancy as to how much money it was. Anyway, Artie asked me to tag along. We get to the restaurant and it's right across the street from the water, you know, where all the fishing boats be docked. When we get out the car I remember there was a guy outside the restaurant smoking a cigarette. I remember having an uneasy feeling about this guy, it felt as if he was waiting for us.

"However, the guy never so much as looked in our direction. So, we go inside the restaurant and it's dim inside. There's a few people here and there, but for the most part the place was deserted. I told Artie right then and there that I had a bad feeling about that place, but Artie told me to relax. Apparently, he'd been dealing with these people long enough to be comfortable, but me? I was a nervous wreck. I would've felt better if we had back up. Anyway, someone comes and escorts us to a table, this guy had to be 90 years old! When we get to the table there's two wise guys already seated and they're both smoking cigars. This is the first time I set eyes on Anthony Orena. In retrospect, my first impression was that he was extremely powerful, I knew he was the boss off the bat! Don't ask me how, but I knew. He stood as we approached the table, a real gentleman, and he offered us to sit down. So, me and Artie, we take a seat. When we sat down I immediately began coughing because of the smoke...

Anthony Orena says, "What's the matter with you? The smoke bothering you? Carmine, put dat cigar out, you're killing dis guy!"

"Thank you!" John O' Conner said in between his coughing fits. His eyes were watery so he dabbed at them with a handkerchief.

They both crushed the burning part of the cigars into an ashtray and Anthony Orena waved the smoke away.

"Is that better?" The Mob Boss asked.

"Yes, thank you! I'm okay."

"Joey, bring these guys something to drink. What are you having?" Anthony Orena asked politely.

That's when Arthur Mullaney decided to take control of the meeting.

"Listen, forget about the drinks! Let's take care of business," Artie said. "Carmine, you have 250 grand for me, I just want what's rightfully mine," he declared with hostility.

"Like hell I owe you a quarter mill! You delivered on one job, that's what you get paid for!" Carmine spit back.

"Listen here you little grease ball" Artie started, but he was interrupted by Anthony Orena.

"Artie please, this is my place. Let's deal with this like gentlemen."

"I agree!" Artie said. "But, Carmine here is the one not being a gentleman about this."

"This guy is crazy if he thinks he's getting 250 large for one job," Carmine said, standing firm on his position.

"It was two jobs, greaseball! You asked me to locate Peter Simon, I located him! You asked me to track down Winston Carter, I tracked him down! I gave you everything you asked for on both these guys. Now I want my money!"

John O'Conner saw that things were getting out of hand, so he attempted to ease the tension by tapping Artie on the back and asking him to relax.

"The only thing, Dick!" Carmine spat with venom. "Is that we never got to use that information."

Artie tried to leap on Carmine but John O'Conner was too quick. He was able to restrain his friend.

"Who the hell you think you're talking to?" Artie yelled in rage.

"Calm down! Control yourself, Artie," John O'Conner pleaded, but his plea fell on deaf ears.

"Artie, you're out of order," Anthony Orena said in a low but deadly tone.

"No, you're out of order!" Artie yelled, disrespecting the boss.

Anthony Orena glanced to his right and someone appeared in the shadows, lurking, just waiting for the command.

"Listen to me, Artie," Anthony Orena started, turning his attention back to Artie and Carmine. "What we have here is a misunderstanding. It's not about da money. Before we were able to use the information you's gave us on Peter Simon, he packed his family up and moved. It would be unreasonable to expect guys like us to pay for information that we was unable to use. Please let's be reasonable about this, Artie."

"Reasonable my ass!" Artie began.

Anthony Orena glanced to his left. Someone was at the table now. It was the man who had been smoking the cigarette in front of the restaurant. Before Artie was able to continue what he was saying someone came behind him and secured a garrote around his neck.

Before John O'Conner could try something stupid, the cold barrel of a pistol was pressed against the side of his face.

He was forced to watch his friend struggle in vain in a futile attempt at escaping the Angel of Death. In under a minute, Artie's face turned beet red as his circulation was cut off, and his mouth opened and closed as if he was in the middle of a heated argument. Only there were no words, just a sickening gurgling sound.

John O'Conner closed his eyes and tried to wish himself to another place, far away, as Arthur Mullaney's life was being drained from his body. When John O'Conner opened his eyes again two guys were dragging Artie's body away from the table, and Anthony Orena was lighting another cigar. The gun was still pressed to John's head and now another person was on his other side.

"*Whadda you want us to do with this one, Boss?*" *One of the flunkies asked.*

Anthony Orena sat back and blew O's in John's direction.

"*I dunno, dat depends,*" *he said as he stared at the crooked detective.*

Anthony Orena reached down and grabbed a bag from the floor. He tossed it on the table.

"*Dat's 125 grand, dat's all we owe you guys. If you're smart you'll take it, if not... you'll end up like your friend. If you take my money and den decide that you wanna blow da whistle, all of Artie's dirty deeds will be revealed, he'll look like a schmuck! If you keep your mouth shut, someone will fill out a missing persons complaint and we all continue on with our lives.*

"*Listen to me, if you think I like this, you're wrong. I hate problems. But everything is about respect. I respect you, you respect me. Your friend made over a million dollars with us! You think I deserve someone coming into my place with disrespect? Of course not! Take da money. It's John O'Conner, right? Good, I asked Artie to bring you along. You and dat partner of yours, Bill Doherty, I've been kept abreast on you guys. You keep your hands in the cookie jar, but you only get da crumbs. I'm gonna make it so you can make some decent money. Enough to send your kids to college, enough to make you appreciate life a little more, and enough to make you respect me. Because, if you don't respect me, John, I'll kill you! If you ever try to cross me and put me behind bars, I'll find you, and I'll kill your family while you watch, just like you watched Artie! Don't fuck with me, and I'll make sure this story has a happy ending... Go 'head take the money."*

John O'Conner was scared to death. He was scared, but he wasn't stupid. He took the money. He took the money, kept his mouth shut, and he and Anthony Orena enjoyed a lucrative partnership.

The Commissioner and the agents in the room watched John O'Conner intently.

"I didn't sleep for three days after the incident," John O'Connor claimed. "And when I was finally able to sleep, I had nightmares. I still have nightmares!" John explained, hoping for sympathy.

Harry Copeland looked over at one of the agents and said, "Clarence, call Judge Stevens. We're going to need a warrant for the arrest of Anthony Orena. And someone place a call to our office in Nevada. I want to give them a heads up." He looked at another agent. "Patrick, call your wife and tell her you won't be coming home tonight. We're taking a trip to Las Vegas!"

CHAPTER ELEVEN

I'm in front of the house.

Chandar looked at the message on his two-way pager and realized he was running late.

"Boo listen, I don't have time for this right now," he told Karen as he straightened his tie. "You know I love you, but I'm running late. And you know it's important that we get these contracts signed and close this deal."

Karen marched into the bathroom of their master bedroom and Chandar followed her.

"Boo, why you acting like that? You know you're not being fair," he pleaded.

"Don't talk to me about fair, Chandar. If closing that deal is more important than me, just go."

"Whoa! Where's all this coming from? I wanted you to be by my side tonight, and you told me that you didn't feel good, so—"

"And you're just going to leave me, and you know I'm not feeling well?"

Chandar grabbed Karen and pulled her to him gently, being conscious of her protruding stomach. He stroked her chin with his forefinger. "Boo, there's nothing in this world that I love or care about more than you, my daughter, or this little guy you're carrying around," he said.

Karen leaned her head on Chandar's shoulder. A feeling of guilt crept in.

"Now, I'm no longer in Vegas so we don't have that income to depend on anymore. I gotta get this paper, Kay! I need to make sure our future is secure, and I need you to understand that. You hear me?"

Karen nodded her head, and Chandar wiped away a lone tear that escaped from her eye.

"I love you, yo! And I want to be with you until the end of time, but I need you to support what I'm trying to do. Never stop a man from being a man, especially a good one. It'll push him away. You know better than that, right?"

Karen nodded her head again.

"I'm sorry, baby," she said, leaning up to give her man a kiss. "Go do what you gotta do, and I'll be okay until you come back."

"That's my baby momma talking," Chandar joked, stealing a kiss. He took her bottom lip into his teeth and suckled it.

Karen punched him in the arm. "You better stop playing! I wanna be your wife"

"Good things come to those who wait! Come and lock the door."

$$$

Since Chandar moved back to New York, he had been extremely mindful of security. Before leaving the rotten apple, he had managed to dethrone one of the most powerful crews to ever grace the five boroughs. The William Cook Organization. New York underworld was the type of place where grudges were kept for generations. That being the case, there were sure to be some enemies laying in the cut, waiting for the opportunity to get revenge.

Taking no chances, Chandar copped what Brabus North America called a UTV, an Urban Tactical Vehicle. It was, in fact, a heavily modified 2002 S Class Mercedes Benz that had the price tag of a Maybach.

The exterior of the car was triple black. Black tint. Black rims. Glossy black paint. The interior was just as abysmal, with the exception of the red trim lining the leather seats and suede floor mats. A bank of red toggle switches hid beneath the center armrest. One of the switches operated dispensers for an oil slick, which was just below the rear bumper, while another was for a smoke screen. The setup was reminiscent of the British secret agent, James

Bond's Aston Martin DBS. Only, Chandar was a 100% Black American man from the streets.

Instead of relying on heavy armor plating, the UTV was lined with a lightweight Kevlar padding which gave up the same protection as steel, at one-third the weight. The windows were protected by a shatter and blast proof semi-rigid protective coating capable of withstanding multiple rounds at close distance from weapons ranging from a .22 caliber to a .44 magnum.

All of the flashy gadgetry was cool, but the item that convinced Chandar (who was a Porsche man) to pay over $300,000 for a Mercedes Benz had to be the little black box that was capable of shutting down anything wireless within 150 feet. This black box didn't only preclude eavesdropping devices, but more importantly, the detonation of explosive devices in or near the car.

Chandar didn't anticipate ever needing to use the added protection, but he had a peace of mind just knowing it was available.

The ghetto star hopped in the whip and pulled up alongside of a green Bentley GT that sat with its engine running in front of the house.

Chandar tapped the horn twice and signaled for Infra-red to follow him. Then, he pumped the volume to full blast and allowed Raekwon's lyrics to take him there.

'Now Yo, Yo! What up, Yo? Time is running out/ it's for real though, let's connect politics, Ditto/ We could trade places, get lifted in the staircases/ Word up, peace to incarcerated scarfaces!'

The luxury vehicles floated through the streets of Long Island, making their way to the Southern Parkway. Their destination was the Nottington Townhouse, a small club in Jamaica, Queens. Jeff White was meeting them there for the signing of the purchase agreement for Loud Mouth Records, and afterward they planned on a small celebration.

'Thug related style attract millions, fans they understand my plan/ Who's the kid up in the green Land?'

Raekwon the Chef's classic *'Only Built for Cuban Links* was the CD of choice as Chandar tried to go into a zone and escape the pressure of once again becoming a father, and possibly even a married man.

"One step at a time, Playboy!" He thought aloud as he maneuvered the V at high speed. The Benz also had laser detectors to alert him when the Law was monitoring speed.

'But yo, guess who's the black Trump?'

Loud Mouth Records would serve as the vehicle to take the team to yet another level. Chandar already had enough money stashed away to live comfortably for the rest of his life, but doing business was his drug of choice. He enjoyed learning the mechanics and what it would take to make a mediocre business into a huge success.

When the ghetto star turned into the parking lot of the club, he found himself behind a gold Range Rover that was infested with four chicks that appeared to be dimes.

He pulled into a parking space right next to them, and Infra-red pulled into a space on the other side of them creating a luxury sandwich. Chandar killed the engine of the Benz. That's when he noticed Infra-red had lowered the window to the Bentley and let his music flood out into the night.

'Peep the script, peeped honey from the whip/ jumped out like Yo! Who the fuck you with?'

Infra-red left the system bangin' for a minute because it seemed like Jigga was already putting things in their right perspective.

'Flash the jewels cause that's the rules...'

Chandar jumped out the whip at the same time the ladies were unloading from the Range. An assortment of tropical smells blessed his nose, complimenting the beautiful women in his presence.

Chandar caught eye contact with one shorty that he thought resembled the model, Melyssa Ford.

The Big Homie was on automatic! "Your face seems familiar, have we met before?" Chandar asked.

Baby girl's smile was like sunshine. "I don't think so ... I would've remembered you," she responded with a sexy ass voice.

"You know who you look like?" Chandar asked. "The model, Jessica Rabbit."

Infra-red met up with them as they walked toward the club.

"Thank you," shorty told Chandar. "That's actually my homegirl."

"J.B.???" A cinnamon-complexioned honey in a sequined dress that molested her curvaceous body was looking at Infra-red as if she couldn't believe her eyes.

Infra-red had stopped too, he was trying to place the face. "It had to be a long ass time ago if you're calling me J.B.," Infra-red said, searching his mental rolodex of women for recognition. Finally, her face (or maybe it was the body) registered. "Candy?"

"Yes!"

"Damn girl, your little ass done grew up!" Infra-red said, marveling at the transformation.

Candy did a slow spin. "Did you think I would stay little forever?" She asked innocently.

"Hell no! Even when you was younger that body was bangin'! Come 'ere and give me a hug." He pulled her into a tight embrace.

"Y'all can get a room later," one of Candy's friends quipped. "For now, let's go up in here and get our party on."

"That sounds like a plan to me," Infra-red said. As they made their way inside the club, he was holding Candy around her waist.

The Nottington Townhouse was a small and cozy club, and on this occasion, all the guest were 'Invite Only' so it was a select crowd. Music executives, rap and R&B artists, and models dominated the environment.

One of the first people that Chandar encountered was Willie Black, an up and coming rapper from a group known as the 4-1-0 Hustlers.

"Chandar, what's good?" Willie Black greeted with a friendly smile.

"It's all about you, Playboy," Chandar responded, giving Willie Black a firm handshake.

"Nah, it's all about you," he returned. "You know what, Chandar? I admire you!" Willie Black said seriously.

Thinking that this was his way of congratulating him on buying the label, Chandar took the compliment lightly. "No doubt! You know, you're still gonna be a priority. My team is gonna take this label to another level. Dr. Hyde is gonna be mad he sold it."

Willie Black's face contorted into a mask of confusion. "Dr. Hyde sold Loud Mouth???"

Now it was Chandar's turn to look confused. "Damn, you didn't know? He must've been planning on surprising you."

"Yeah, I'm surprised alright. That's some real sucka shit!"

"Whoa, Player! You making it sound like you don't got faith in me," Chandar pointed out, clearly offended by the remark.

"Nah, it ain't that. But that nigga could've at least told somebody he was selling the label. I got over 300 grand put away!"

"If it'll make you feel better," Chandar said. "Three-hundred grand ain't even 3% of what we paid for the label."

With perfect timing, Del Gibson spotted Chandar. He and Jeff White made their way over.

"There you go, it took you long enough," Dr. Hyde said. He gave Chandar dap and a manly hug.

Without warning, Willie Black stormed off!

"What the hell is wrong with him?" Jeff White asked feeling the tension.

"I think he had to take a shit!" Chandar said.

Dr. Hyde wasn't concerned with none of that. He was used to Willie Black's charades. "Come on, we're upstairs!" he said, leading the way to the celebration.

$$$

'So, tell me wheeeeeere ...where will you gooooo? And whooooo, who's gonna love you like I doooo...'

The words of Babyface were soothing, yet depressing. Karen sought to challenge her ambivalence by being optimistic. However, her situation turned out, it wouldn't be the end of the world.

She was curled up on the couch eating Chunky Monkey ice cream, vibing on the 'Tender Lover' CD when the phone rang. Karen was on point, she had everything important to her in arm's reach so she wouldn't have to wobble around the house. She had the house phone, her cell phone, her pocketbook (which held a snub nosed .38 revolver in it), and of course, the remote control for everything. She planned to eat her ice cream in peace and just chill. No interruptions.

After checking the caller I.D., she had to take this call.

"What's good, Sis?" Karen said, trying to sound as if she was in high spirits.

Karen's sister, Regina, was responsible for handling the day-to-day affairs at Karen's Soul Food restaurant while Karen was out on maternity leave.

"Nothing. I just called to get on your nerves and see how you're doing. I have to make sure that gangsta boyfriend of yours doesn't have you tied up somewhere," Regina joked, laughing hysterically.

"Ha, Ha! You need to take your show on the road, you are too funny," Karen said sarcastically. "Is everything in order at the restaurant?"

Regina understood this to mean that her sister was in a sour mood.

"Well, the delivery truck was supposed to bring the soda since Tuesday, and we're getting low. I called and they said it'll be here tomorrow, but that's bad business!"

"You call them back tomorrow, whether the delivery comes or not, and you ask to speak to Mr. Patterson, the plant manager. You tell him if this shit happens again, we're searching for a new distributor. Bottom line! Now, are any of the workers giving you a hard time? Are they listening to you?"

"Everything else is fine. You know Suzette comes in when she wants to, but—"

"Regina, if that bitch comes in late again you dock her ass! Take it out her check, shit, she wouldn't do that if she was working for them white people!" Karen yelled. Her phone beeped indicating someone was on the other line. She looked at the caller I.D. and said, "Listen, the phone just beeped and I have to take this call, so I'll talk to you tomorrow, okay?"

"Okay, I love you!"

"Love you, too!"

Karen clicked to the other line.

"Hey Jada!"

"Hey! What you doing?"

"I was talking to my crazy ass sister! Girl, I'll be glad when I get back to work."

"I hear that," Jada said. "But if you know what I know, you'll enjoy the vacation."

"True! Where your bad ass son at?"

"In the bed, thank God! His little ass is driving me crazy. I'll be glad when his father comes home."

"I bet you will," Karen said with a laugh.

"Pa-leeeze! I'm not thinking about that boy. I told you he had the next bitch on the visit when I went up there. He had the nerve to tell me that she was just bringing him some damn drugs. Yeah right!"

"I didn't know about that!" Karen screamed.

"These niggas think we're supposed to be so stupid. I don't even wanna talk about his ass though. Did you think about what we talked about?"

"When?"

"About the baby."

Karen got quiet. She knew what Jada was referring to now.

Jada sensed that Karen was uneasy, so she spoke for her, "We don't have to talk about it, but if I was you, I would keep my mouth shut. What Chandar don't know won't hurt him."

Karen wished it was that easy. Making a man believe that he was the father of a child that wasn't his was some real foul shit. So many women used this trick until it was almost common, but Karen didn't think she would be able to live with such a dirty secret. Fuck the man; it wouldn't be fair to the child!

"I don't know, Jada. I don't think I can go through with it. Besides, I think Chandar may be understanding – he's like my soulmate. If I don't tell him and he finds out down the line, then what?"

"If you tell him now, then what???" Jada shot back.

"Then he'll take a paternity test," Karen stated.

"And if the baby's not his what do you think he's going to do?"

"I don't know!!!" Karen yelled. "I don't fucking know, Jada! What am I supposed to do?"

Jada let a moment of silence hang before she responded. "Keep your mouth shut, Karen. What Chandar don't know won't hurt him."

Karen heard Jada loud and clear, but deep down she wasn't so convinced.

$$$

After the signing of the contract that transferred the ownership of Loud Mouth Records, Del Gibson had some festivities lined up. He was with Jeff White, Chandar, and their respective counsel on the balcony overlooking the small dance floor and makeshift stage. With a prearranged hand signal, things were set in motion.

Toylin and Tequan, biological sisters from the label's R&B group, Dimes, approached the stage. The lights were dimmed and the spotlight focused on the two beautiful women as they stood before the crowd.

"How y'all doing?" Toylin asked the crowd enthusiastically.

The crowd erupted, especially the tables that held Tee and Toy's friends and family.

"We just wanna wish Del Gibson a farewell. It's been wonderful working with you," Tequan proclaimed.

"And we wanna welcome Jeff White and Chandar to the family!" Toylin added.

The crowd applauded!

"We have to thank our family for coming out and supporting us. Rosa, Lydia, Kofi, Jessica, Jamese, and Jada! Nika and John Tarik—Thank you!" Tequan said.

"And we want to sing a song for you. This song is dedicated to a very special person, Luisa Henry. Rest in peace Mommy—WE LOVE YOU." Toylin whispered respectfully into the microphone.

The instrumental from the classic Kool and the Gang song, *Cherish* wafted through the room. The crowd nodded their heads in anticipation of the smooth banger, until Tequan began to sing.

Her voice was smoother than silk as she belted out the tunes:

"Let's take a walk together, near the ocean shore... hand and hand you and I."

(Toylin) "Let's cherish every moment, we have been given... Before it pass us by!"

(Tequan) "I often pray, before I laaay down—"

(Toylin) "By your side,"

(Tequan) "If you receive your calling, before I awake,"

(Toylin) "Could I make it through the niiight?"

(Tee & Toy) "Cherish the love we have, we should cherish the life we live..."

(Tequan) "Cherish the life,"

(Toylin) "Cherish the life."

(Tee & Toy) "Cherish the life!"

Dimes captivated the audience and controlled the energy in the club! When they finished performing the people were on their feet applauding and whistling. A few family members were actually crying.

The 4-1-0 Hustlers were supposed to perform also, but Willie Black was buckin'. He was still mad about being the last one to find out that Dr. Hyde was selling the label. So instead of the 4-1-0-Hustlers performing, Cub did a solo performance and put the crowd back in high spirits.

While the crowd awaited the next performer, Infra-red was at a table with Candy playing catch up. He learned that baby girl was a model, and not only was she in a few rap videos, but she did a spread for King Magazine!

"Ayo! That's what's up!" Infra-red congratulated her on her accomplishments. "I'm proud of you, Boo. Now all you need is a good nigga to lock that ass down."

"I'm too busy to be letting somebody lock this down," Candy said. Then, on second thought, she added, "Unless of course, the right one comes along."

"I hear that hot shit! Ayo, how's your mom doing?" Infra-red asked, ducking the last comment.

"Not too good. Peggy is smoking crack."

"Damn, word? I'm sorry to hear that," Infra-red said, shaking his head. Ms. Peggy was the last person he would expect to be riding the dragon, but hey, it happened to the best of them. "I still would like to see her, I could at least try to help."

"You can only help someone who's willing to help their self."

"That's true," Infra-red agreed. He dropped the subject and casually glanced around the club for the exit. "You ready to get up out of here?"

Candy smiled. "I thought you was scared to ask."

"Imagine that!" Infra-red said, laughing. "I'll be right back."

Infra-red went to holla at Chandar while Candy went to tell her girlfriends that she was leaving.

Chandar and Infra-red were actually on the same page because Chandar was contemplating leaving with one of Candy's friends. However, when it was all said and done, the ghetto star changed his mind. He had a beautiful woman waiting for him at home, and she was pregnant with a child, his child.

Chandar informed Jeff White and Dr. Hyde that he was leaving. As he neared the exit, the area was so congested that he bumped into one of the guests that stood with their back turned. Chandar prepared to offer an apology as the man turned around, but instead, the ghetto star got the shock of the night! To Chandar's dismay, he found himself staring face-to-face with the last person on the planet he expected to see.

Standing there, waiting for a reaction, was none other than Jesse James.

He was also known as A-Blood.

CHAPTER TWELVE

His reputation proceeded him. And while it was unequivocal that Reggie Ransom had a lack of regard for human life, his sick mind would reason that there was a method to his madness. To those fortunate (or unfortunate) enough to befriend the killer, Reggie Ransom wasn't a bad fella. In fact, most of the people who knew him refused to believe the horrific stories that circulated about the O.G.

Tasha was one of those people who didn't believe that Reggie Ransom and the Grim Reaper were one in the same. It was impossible, in her mind, for such a kind and gentle old man to actually be the crazy and deranged individual known as the Grim Reaper, or One Shot, as he was called in some circles. O.G. was a good person! This is why Tasha felt comfortable talking to Reggie about her relationship with Peanut. He listened intently whenever she spoke to him in confidence, every now and then nodding his head in understanding.

"What I don't understand is this, Tasha..." Reggie said to her one day while they talked in front of her house. "Why is everybody saying that he's a snitch? If it's true, then he's putting you in danger because somebody is gonna mess around and come after him. And when they do, you and I both know that bullets don't have names on them."

"He's not a snitch! People are just jealous of Peanut," Tasha insisted, in her man's defense.

"See, that's why you're my road dawg. And believe me, you're not doing nothing wrong—you're supposed to defend your man," Reggie said. "But listen to me, there's no way anybody is gonna get busted with drugs and then come home the same night. It just don't work like that."

"And you know what?" Tasha said, cutting Reggie off. "I asked him about that. What people fail to realize is that Peanut know a lot of people. And he only got caught with what, 2 or 3 grams of crack at the most?"

Reggie Ransom appeared to be amused, "What does knowing a lot of people have to do with this?"

Tasha sucked her teeth, "It's not *what* you know, Reggie, it's *who* you know! Peanut's people got him out of jail—that's why he was home that same night," Tasha said this as if she was stating an obvious fact, like it was as simple as 1+1.

"Oh yeah?" Reggie asked, playing along as if he was impressed. "Peanut connected like that? Who's his people?"

"Well, I don't know them personally. I mean, all I know is this—Peanut came home talking about the star in the mirror..."

Tasha kept talking, but the Grim Reaper didn't hear anything she said after she mentioned the star in the mirror. Reggie Ransom was ready to kill again. That day it felt as if the star in the mirror was closing in on him.

About an hour earlier, he had just finished engaging Teddy's girlfriend, Tonya, in conversation—and she also had mentioned the star in the mirror. That was enough to send the O.G. into action, and consequently, both Peanut and Teddy were murdered. Guilty by association!

Now Reggie Ransom sat in the back of a cab driving through the streets of Jamaica, Queens searching for something to get into. Ever since the big homie Jerry Moore had been kidnapped by the federal government, Reggie was only able to survive by means of extortion and robbery. He was putting his hard and soft extortion game down on drug dealers and stick up kids. The soft extortion game was this: "Road-Dawg, I'm fucked up—let a nigga hold something."

And hard extortion meant that somebody was tied up or handcuffed in the trunk of a vehicle, or in a dark basement of a home in a remote location where no one would hear the screams of agony that penetrated dark nights.

"Make a left turn on 118th Avenue," Reggie told 6A.

6A was one of the Grim Reapers personal cab drivers from A &B cab stand. He drove a burgundy Toyota Camry. Everyone in the 'hood knew that 6A was an old gangsta. He was well respected in his younger days, and even in old age he knew how to mind his business. 6A's motto was the same thing that allowed him to survive and thrive. It was simple: "I don't know shit! I didn't see nothing. I didn't hear nothing—just pay me what you owe me."

As a result, 6A was the getaway driver on countless occasions as culprits fled various crime scenes.

6A made the left turn on 118th avenue and Reggie Ransom surveyed the surroundings until he spotted Tasha sitting on the stoop in front of her house talking to one her girlfriends. He instructed 6A to pull over. When the car stopped he jumped out to holla at shorty.

"Road dawg, what's up with you? You tryna hide from me or something?"

Tasha couldn't believe her eyes! She couldn't believe that Reggie Ransom had the audacity to show his face in her neighborhood, let alone try to talk to her as if everything was cool. Shorty flipped!

"Get the fuck away from my house! Don't come near me!" She screamed.

Reggie Ransom froze in his tracks with a confused look on his face. Even Tasha's girlfriend was startled by her friend's outburst.

"Go! Before I call the cops, you murderer!" Tasha spat before she broke down and started crying.

Her friend put an arm around her shoulder and tried to comfort her, or at least calm her down.

"Road dawg, you got it wrong—I didn't kill nobody," The Grim Reaper said sincerely. He was putting on an Oscar-worthy performance.

"You did! Everybody knows you killed Peanut—and I trusted you!" Tasha cried.

"Baby girl, listen to me, I was with Sabrina and her friends when that shit happened. All you gotta do is ask. I swear on my mother's grave I didn't kill that boy," Reggie swore, trying to convince Tasha that she was wrong.

"So, why they lying on you then? Why is everybody saying that you killed my man? Why Reggie?"

The Grim Reaper shook his head from side to side, apologetic for not knowing the answer. Then, it came to him.

"People don't know what they be talking about, Road dawg. The streets always gonna spread rumors. They even lied on Peanut, may he rest in peace. When he was alive they was saying he was a snitch, but you and I both know that wasn't true."

Tasha looked at Reggie Ransom as if what he said made a whole lot of sense.

"You can call Sabrina and ask her where I was when Peanut got killed, but it's still messed up that you would even believe I would do something like that. I never had no problems with Peanut. But you know what Road Dawg? Maybe I shouldn't have even came to check on you. If I'm wrong for that, then I apologize, and you don't never have to worry about seeing me again."

Reggie Ransom spun off and began to walk away. He barely took five steps when Tasha's voice stopped him.

"Reggie wait!" She got up and ran to him. "I'm sorry! I don't know what to believe –"

"Shhhh...it's okay, Road Dawg. Everything is gonna be alright. I'm here for you." The Grim Reaper held her in his arms while rocking back and forth. This was part of the job that he hated the most. Consoling the victims left behind from the victims he left behind.

After getting Tasha to calm down, they sat together on her stoop and Reggie began to press her for useful information she could provide. He wanted to know who was saying that he killed Peanut. What were Big Time and Kool-Aid saying? Where did Big Time and Kool-Aid live? Reggie told Tasha that he wanted to do his own investigation and find out what really happened to Peanut, but in reality, Reggie Ransom wanted to know who had his name in their mouth so he could make the guilty parties disappear.

The only reason he wanted to find Big Time was because word on the street was that the kid was seeing major paper. Either Big Time was gonna set it out, or Big Time was going in the trunk of 6A's Camry.

The Grim Reaper's motive for wanting to locate Kool-Aid was to congratulate him on doing a good job with Peanut, and maybe even try to recruit him for future jobs.

By the time Reggie Ransom departed from Tasha's stoop he had his work cut out for him. Tasha had provided more than enough Information. If he could only find Teddy's girlfriend, Tonya, his mission would be complete.

As they slid through the Queens streets, 6A broke the silence, "Hey man, where you tryna go?"

The Grim Reaper read the address off of the crumpled piece of paper in his hand. If Big Time was home, he was in for a big surprise.

$$$

It was a Friday night on I-63. The Big Homie was in his cell with Barkim and Shan Will about to smoke some trees. On the street Jerry Moore didn't even smoke weed, but his present situation was sometimes hard to cope with. As a result, the Big Homie found himself looking for different ways to escape. Most times he would bury himself in law work, reading and shephardizing case law, filing motions, and searching for loop holes to help him win his case. Sometimes he played chess, or he would watch CNN to see what was going on in the world. And then there were times like this when the Big Homie would smoke some trees or get drunk off the wine somebody cooked up using fruit juices, yeast, and sugar—this was the concoction that the prisoners called, *Hooch!*

"Ayo! That shit smell exotic," Shan Will said, sniffing the air as he watched Barkim roll a Phillie Blunt.

"Ole' girl said that's that strawberry hydro," Jerry Moore informed him, referring to the weed that he got from Ms. Ballard.

Ms. Ballard was a Corrections Officer that worked the 7a.m.-3p.m. shift on the unit. She was from East New York and shorty was infatuated with thug ass niggaz! Once she got the run down on Jerry Moore she did just about anything he asked her to do short of helping him escape.

"Wait 'til I put some fire to this shit, watch how it smell then," Barkim said, pulling out a lighter and firing up.

Jerry Moore took a swig of the hooch he was nursing and then passed it to Shan Will.

"You hear me, Big Homie?" Shan Will said. "This shit got me fucked up already."

"I don't know why you getting Shan Will drunk, you know that nigga can't hold his liquor," Barkim said as he took a long drag and held in the smoke.

"You buggin' son, why you say I can't hold my liquor?" Shan Will asked, sounding as if he was offended.

"Because," Barkim paused to take another long drag. "Last time you got drunk, you was going around the unit slapping niggaz for nothing."

"Nigga pass the blunt!" Jerry Moore barked.

Barkim snapped his head toward the Big Homie and quickly passed the blunt, "Oh! My bad nigga, that shit was tasting good like a muthafucka."

Shan Will was sipping on the hooch staring at Barkim. He didn't like the thought he couldn't hold his liquor.

"I only slapped two people, and that was 'cause they was being nosey. You act like I slapped four or five people."

"You hear this fool?" Barkim asked. "He only slapped two people. You better leave these hot ass niggaz alone before they fuck around and give you a new case for fucking with government witnesses."

Jerry Moore went into a coughing fit and Barkim patted him on the back. When he stopped coughing he gritted on Barkim. "Both of y'all niggaz shut the fuck up, and somebody look out the door and see where the police at," he said.

Barkim crept over to the door and peeped out the small rectangular shaped window. "That nigga way up front talking on the phone dawg. Let me find out you paranoid."

"Imagine that! I know one thing, this 'dro got me feeling like my wheelchair is floating."

Barkim broke out laughing while Jerry Moore passed the blunt to Shan Will.

"Y'all buggin," Shan Will said. He took the 'dro and went to the head.

For the rest of the night niggaz was listening to their radios. Hot 97 FM was rocking like crazy! Barkim made his famous Tuna Fish hook up while Shan Will and Jerry Moore traded war stories to pass the time. This scenario became routine, and days and weeks passed by like the scenery does when you're in a moving vehicle.

At times, Jerry Moore analyzed his cruel reality and his heart was filled with hatred. Jerry Moore was facing the death penalty if he blew trial, but the government left two options available to him. Accept a plea agreement with the government and receive a Life sentence, or cooperate with the government and receive an equally devastating 30-year prison term.

To the Big Homie, the two options weren't options at all. "We could start picking right now!" He would say arrogantly, referring to the process of picking a jury, which was necessary to begin trial.

But the truth was, the Big Homie was afraid. This was typical because, no sane person would want to die by lethal injection, nor would any sane person look forward to spending the rest of their life behind barbed wired fences. This was the perfect time for Jerry Moore to ask himself: *Was it really worth it?*

A natural occurrence when a person is in trouble is that they turn to God in whichever way they understand him. This is exactly what Jerry Moore began to do. He began secretly reading the Bible, and found peace reading Psalms and Proverbs. One of his favorite stories was the story of Job! The Big Homie read that story again and again, and found inspiration each time.

Late at night while everyone was sleeping, Jerry Moore would be up having private conversations with God. Instead of asking God to help him get out of jail, he begged God to give him faith like Job and to help him understand his purpose in life. He asked God for good health and to allow his legs to heal properly so he could walk again.

One day, the Big Homie was lounging in his cell reading his Bible when Shan Will tapped on the door and walked in the room. Jerry Moore quickly tucked the small Bible under his leg hoping Shan Will didn't see it, but the little homie was on point like an arrow.

"What's poppin', Big Homie?" Shan Will said, greeting his boss.

"Moreless, it be blood poppin' and foes dropping. You already know!" Jerry Moore said spitting that slick shit and grabbing his radio off the bed as if he was about to go watch T.V. or something.

"Why you put your Bible away? I hope I didn't disturb you," Shan Will said catching the Homie off guard. Shan Will had a childlike voice that sounded innocent.

"Fuck is you talking 'bout?" Jerry Moore asked, playing dumb.

"Nah, I saw you put your Bible away when I came in. I'm just saying ain't nothing wrong with reading the Bible. My favorite book is Ecclesiastics."

"Oh yeah?" The Big Homie said looking at Shan Will with a smirk.

On the streets, these fools sold drugs, robbed people, and committed murder. Jerry Moore was amazed that a person like Shan Will even believed in God, let alone had a favorite book in the Bible. Yet, it wasn't just prison that compelled a person to seek out the Lord of all Worlds. Many difficulties and calamities forced people to cry out and beg for mercy. Shan Will and Jerry Moore were no exception.

"I was just reading Job," Jerry Moore admitted. "Ole' boy lost everything but he still had faith. Even his wife was trippin', she wanted him to curse God—"

"And Job called her a foolish woman!" Shan Will interjected with a smile.

Jerry Moore smiled too. He was still amazed that the little homie was no stranger to the stories in the Bible.

"Job had everything. Good health, an abundance of wealth, a wife and kids, and he had honor amongst the people. Then just like that –" Jerry Moore snapped his fingers. "It was gone!"

Shan Will knew that the Big Homie was comparing the story of Job with his own situation. Truth be told though, their present situation to the tenth power wouldn't come close to the hardships that Job had to endure.

So, the little homie said, "But...Job was patient, and he put his trust in God. And in the end, God gave him back his health, and even more possessions than he had the first time."

While the two gangstas sat contemplating the lessons from the story of Job, Barkim came barging in the room.

"Ayo! Your co-defendants are at the door. They said come to the law library."

Barkim went to his locker and grabbed his prison I.D. card.

"They called it already?" Shan Will asked.

"Yeah, yeah. He called it just now," Barkim said.

Just then G-Bundles and Cue came barging in the room.

"Come on Big Homie, come to the library for an hour so we can chill with you," Cue yelled and then kissed Jerry Moore on the forehead.

G-Bundles was peeking out the window. "Hurry up 'cause that sucker ass cop is looking for us!" he said sounding out of breath.

"Come on Shan Will, what y'all waiting for?" Cue prodded.

Jerry Moore grabbed his I.D. and a net bag of law work and they were out the door.

$$$

Reggie Ransom camped out across the street from Big Time's house for three hours in the back seat of 6A's Toyota Camry before he finally gave up and told 6A to drop him off in Brooklyn.

Had Big Time showed up, he would've been a victim of Reggie Ransom's hard extortion! He would've been tied up and tortured, and 9 times out of 10 he would've been killed. Still, the Grim Reaper wasn't a terrible person. He was just tired and frustrated. After a good night's rest, he would probably reconsider and allow Big Time the opportunity to submit to the soft extortion.

On his drive back to Brooklyn, the Grim Reaper thought about Jerry Moore. He felt bad for the Big Homie and wished there was more he could do to help him. He was already doing the best he could by eliminating any and all possible witnesses, but he still wished he could do more. He made a mental note to get in touch with the other Big Homie. Reggie Ransom was actually trying to lay low because he didn't want to draw unnecessary heat to his team, but he concluded it was time. It was time to check in with the Boss!

153

Tomorrow, he would contact Chandar.

CHAPTER THIRTEEN

Baby girl had a swagger that was bananas! It was the week after the signing of the contract that transferred ownership of Loud Mouth Records to Jeff White, and they were having an executive meeting at the label's headquarters. It was actually a little of both, business and pleasure, because although Chandar ordered the entire staff to be present at this meeting, there was also a banquet set up. Add to that the ever-present bottles of champagne chilling in buckets of ice all throughout the studios and the vibe was almost like the celebration after winning a championship.

The up and coming R&B group, Dimes, flew back from L.A. where they had just completed an elaborate photo shoot. BJ was the A&R assigned to the sisters, and he had already navigated them through various key stages. They had over twenty songs recorded and the only thing they were waiting for now was a new budget to be approved so they could begin marketing their first single, a lady's anthem called, *I Can Please Myself*.

Willie Black and the 4-1-0 Hustlers were in the building, as was their manager Vinnie Garrett. The 4-1-0 Hustlers had put out two of the hottest mixtapes in the city, and although they had done numerous guest appearances on other established artists' projects, they had yet to get the green light to drop their own highly-anticipated debut album. Willie Black's main objective was to become first priority at Loud Mouth. Anything other than that, and he wanted out of his contract.

One of the most sought-after producers in the industry, Maxwell Smart, was in attendance. The Super Producer had everyone bobbing their heads as one of his bangin' instrumentals penetrated the premises.

Chandar had Karen by his side looking radiant, big belly and all, and each person in the Ghetto star's inner circle had permission to bring a friend along if they were inclined to do so. Makavelli, Corleone, and Wild Blood declined the offer to bring a friend, but Infra-red invited Candy, and all eyes were on her.

Baby girl had a swagger that was bananas! The Dolce & Gabbana dress she wore exposed her entire back and accentuated every curve on her tantalizingly beautiful body. Spaghetti straps graced her delicate, toned shoulders, and her persona screamed: "I'm the baddest bitch in the building, and I know it!"

Although most of the staff were dressed informally, a sprinkle of men and women sporting business suits blended into the scene as attorneys, book keepers, and accountants waited patiently to discuss consequential matters with the new executive staff, particularly Chandar.

The headquarters of Loud Mouth Records was a spacious entity housed inside the Soul Convention on Merrick Boulevard in Queens, New York. Upon entering the glass doors of the studio's entrance, the first thing you encountered was a glass partition built into the wall, which was right next to a thick steel door that remained locked at all times. The only way to gain entry was to be buzzed in by the secretary.

On the other side of the partition was the secretary's office, and one of the secretary's responsibilities was to memorize the names of the people who were to be granted access to the studios. If a person didn't have an appointment, or their name wasn't logged inside of the computer database, the secretary would make a courtesy call to the staff member or artist that was being sought. Only after receiving approval would the visitor be buzzed in.

Once you made it past the thick steel door, you were officially inside the studios of Loud Mouth Records, AKA "The Dungeon" (as it was affectionately called by those whom regarded the studios as a second home.) To the right was the door to the secretary's office, and next to that was a two-stall bathroom. Straight ahead was a small room that held an ice machine, a soda machine, two vending machines, and on a small round table sat an industrial microwave. To the left of the room was a corridor that led throughout the premises. On the right side of the corridor was an exercise room with free weights, a treadmill, and pull up and dip bars. Then there was a lounge which housed a huge flat screen T.V. with an X-Box, and an assortment of arcade games hugging the walls. On the left side of the corridor were two state-of-the art soundproof recording studios. The first one was marked studio "A", the second one was marked studio "B". Finally, at the end of the corridor was a huge office with its own full bathroom.

This was the office that was formerly used by Del Gibson, and it was a perfect comfort zone for the residential H.N.I.C. (Head Nigga In Charge.) In the middle of the office was a pool table and Chandar was uncertain if it would stay or go. For the time being, the pool table was serving its purpose as Corleone and Wild Blood engaged in a game of 9 ball.

Everyone mingled and flowed freely throughout the offices and studios of Loud Mouth sipping on bubbly, while Chandar expertly controlled the mood. It was a celebration, but business was the first priority.

Standing in a corner of the room embracing Karen from behind, gently rubbing her stomach, Chandar was holding court. He spoke intensely with Gail Grey, his corporate attorney, who was advising him to set up a limited partnership as opposed to a limited liability company. She was explaining the wisdom of such a move when a distinguished looking gentleman caught her attention. The gentleman was dressed immaculately. As the stranger made his way over, Chandar noticed his salt and pepper hair attesting to his age. He had to be in his late fifties, or early sixties.

"Gail Grey," the gentleman said, politely easing into their space. "It's good to see you again. And you must be Chandar?"

Chandar sized the stranger up immediately. He didn't recognize the face, but something told him that this was a person that he was supposed to know.

"Somebody give this man a cigar," Chandar said asserting his presence with a smile.

"I hope I'm not imposing on you guys. My name is Charles, Charles Watlington."

"Charles is into asset protection, Chandar," Gail Grey said, offering some clarity.

"Is that right?" Chandar asked, curious as to the reason that he was just given that information.

"I'm actually a Trust Attorney," Mr. Watlington clarified. He passed Chandar one of his business cards. "I'm the U.S. government's worst nightmare! My clients pay 1% taxes on everything they own, and Uncle Sam can't do shit about it, excuse my language. The IRS can take lessons from me."

Chandar glanced at Gail Grey and saw that she was smiling. Turning his attention back to the man who politely interrupted their meeting, he asked, "And how do you manage to do that, Mr...?"

"Watlington! But you can call me Charles."

"Okay Charles, how do your clients get the privilege of only paying 1% taxes?"

Charles raised his shoulders and looked down at the ground before looking back up. "Wellll...it's not exactly a privilege; it's the law. If you reorganize your business, Chandar, into an Irrevocable Business Trust, not only will you dramatically reduce your liability for taxes, but you'll be afforded real privacy. The irrevocable business trust is impenetrable! It protects from scrutiny, it provides for tax-free exchanges of property, it provides a significant degree of protection from almost all taxes..."

While Charles spoke, Chandar listened attentively. The Big Homie loved to peep game, and what he was hearing now almost sounded too good to be true. He could actually set up a business entity that would be above scrutiny by both the government *and* the public? If this was true, then why wasn't everybody using the irrevocable business trust? Chandar waited until Charles was finished with his spiel, and then asked, "So, what's the catch?"

Karen giggled. She was thinking the same thing, and she looked over her shoulder at her boo to bless him with a smile for asking the million-dollar question.

"Well..." Charles said, looking around the office and then back to Chandar, "There is no catch."

"I'm saying Playboy, if it's as simple as you just explained, why isn't everybody doing it?"

"Let me be blunt, Chandar," Charles paused a moment to figure out the best way to speak his truth. Finally, he just came out with it. "Our people are ignorant! All the white folks use business trusts, mega corporations use them, banks. . . everyone knows the loophole's, except us. That's the problem with negroes, we're not smart with our money. When we get some money the first thing we want to do is buy a Mercedes Benz, and pay high percentages on credit and charge cards. We don't invest our money. We don't protect our assets. You follow me?"

Chandar nodded.

"Now, let me ask you a question. They're over there shooting pool. If one of them balls fly off that table and hit somebody in their head, what you think is going to happen? They're going to sue your ass! Excuse my language. They're going to sue you, they're going to sue your company, they may even sue the city for not having restrictions on pool tables being in offices. A trust would protect you from that! If everything was in a trust, you as an individual would be protected because the trust takes the responsibility. Hell, the record label would be protected because in your situation I would probably set up multiple trusts." Charles counted off on his fingers.

"One trust would actually own the label, and another trust would own all the equipment in here, including this pool table. That way you're isolating liability. If something happens involving the pool table, the trust holding the equipment is responsible, not the C.E.O. of the label, not the label itself."

Chandar interjected. "But if I'm the owner of the trust –"

"There is no owner!" Charles proclaimed, as if it was obvious. "There's trustees and beneficiaries, man! You can make yourself a trustee, or you can be the general manager that deals with the daily affairs

162

of the trust. The beneficiary could be your wife here, or the little baby she's carrying, or both. Either way they can't sue you because technically the trust belongs to the beneficiary, and they can't sue the beneficiary because technically it doesn't belong to them yet. You understand me now?"

"I think I follow you, but I'll tell you what, let's set up a meeting for later on this week. That shit sounds tight, but I need to know exactly what I'm getting into before I go jumping out the window," Chandar concluded, smoothly buying time to check dude out and get a second opinion on this business trust thing.

"How does Thursday sound? Say around 9:30?" Charles asked, eager to secure a new client.

"Thursday is good, but it has to be after twelve. How about 12:30, right here?" Chandar suggested.

"12:30 is good."

Chandar extended his hand and the men shook before Charles Watlington made his smooth departure.

While Chandar conducted business, Makavelli handled his type of business. A chilled glass of champagne in his right hand, Makavelli was bullshitting around on the mic, flowing to the hot beats created by Maxwell Smart. They were in Studio A, and Vinnie was nodding his head to the track. Maxwell Smart knew exactly what Vinnie was looking for, and agreed that a hardcore underground beat would definitely complement Makavelli's flow.

The Dimes were getting their drink on, flossing in the studio like straight divas, but Willie Black had his face screwed up as if he didn't appreciate the next man getting some shine.

Infra-red and Candy had walked in Studio A just in time to hear Makavelli lacing the track Maxwell Smart had dug up. The base line was crazy!

"It's Makavelli, I'm straight from the ghetto/ long time fetish for Dinero/

niggaz say I'm loco/ I still got beef with Po-Po/ and down low cats

that don't tell chicks they homo/ Faggot niggaz don't know- I be holdin'

it down/ When it's poppin' they would know 'cause I'll probably have the black four pound/

But if it's beef right now, I got the Glock right now/ And the morgue, probably got the pine box right now/

164

*That's what you get in the long run, fuckin' with the
wrong one/ Bid your hand son, don't count that strong
one/*

*This ain't spades and I don't renege/ I know cats that
drop buildings and blow up kids/*

*be these same type of fellas, won't do no bids/ and they
don't care if they die, as long as you don't live/*

*They blow Amtrak off the tracks/ Flood the world with
anthrax/ While petty cats still sell crack/ and I can send
you where you can't come back/*

*Where's that? To hell, so leave your money cause there
ain't no bail—"*

Makavelli was going hard, and Infra-red had
sent somebody to get Chandar. By the time the Big
Homie and the rest of the team invaded Studio A,
Makavelli had probably already spit over a hundred
bars and was still going.

*"I spit hotter than the average nigga/ somebody grab this
nigga/ before I spazz and put the mag to niggaz/*

*I spit underground shit, like bullet tag my nigga/ the type
shit that make a nigga say 'damn, my nigga'/*

*Who stacks is bigger? Question is: whose gats is bigger?/
I'm laid back in the cut like relax, my nigga!"/*

*I got this, and niggaz better believe when I drop this hot
shit/ gun in your ass, you still wanna pop shit?/*

Yeah! Makavelli... 150 bars nigga!

Everybody in Studio A was going bananas! No one aside from Corleone even knew Makavelli could flow, let alone go as hard as he just went. Chandar waited until everybody calmed down before he addressed the people.

"Somebody turn that music down, let me get everybody's attention!" The Big Homie said, putting one of his arms around Wild Blood.

When the studio was silent, Chandar began to speak, "Check this shit out, Loud Mouth Records is about to go to a whole 'nother level. I don't know how Del did shit, and I really don't care. As of this moment, you are now looking at the president of Loud Mouth Records... Wild Blood."

Chandar looked at his protégé' to gauge his reaction. Wild Blood couldn't contain the surprised expression on his face. He was smiling and shaking his head in disbelief. He couldn't believe the Big Homie had just put him on the spot like that.

"Vinnie, I want you to be the Vice President," Chandar continued. "Within the next couple of weeks, we should have a new budget worked out so we can get a few projects off the ground. Another thing, I don't care if you're an artist, A & R, a producer, or an intern—Loud Mouth is a family! This shit ain't *my* vision, it's *our* vision. I want y'all to keep that in mind. If anybody has any questions or concerns, y'all holla at Wild Blood or Vinnie. Other than that, everybody eat 'til you're full and drunk, or 'til it's gone. Enjoy the party!"

Before everyone was able to get back to their groove and digest the changing of the guard, Willie Black's voice thundered through the room.

"Whose gonna be first priority?" He was leaning against the mixing board with his clothes slightly disheveled and his mouth twisted at the corner. His bloodshot eyes were directed right at Chandar.

The Big Homie hoped that this silver back looking nigga wouldn't be a problem. The truth was, between Wild Blood, Infra-red, and Corleone alone, they had over twenty confirmed murders. Chandar wasn't trying to boost that count, especially on such a festive night. He opted to try diplomacy.

"Moreless Playboy, you got Vinnie for your manager. Fortunately, he's also the Vice President now. I'm pretty sure 4-1-0 Hustlers will be one of his priorities," Chandar presumed. He peppered his statement with a smile to really drive his point home.

Willie Black wasn't buying it though. "I hope so, because I'm getting sick and tired of this bullshit! If I'm not gonna be priority, I'm outta here."

Wild Blood interjected. "Hit the gas then, nigga! Fuck outta here with that bullshit! Vinnie tear that nigga contract up!" He wasn't about to pussyfoot around. It had to be understood that under the new administration, disrespect or extortion would not be tolerated.

"Tear it up then!" Willie Black yelled, standing up as if he was ready to get it popping.

Vinnie Garrett saw things about to explode and quickly intervened, "Whoa! Everybody calm down. Wild Blood, let me talk to him," Vinnie pleaded, pulling Willie Black toward the exit.

"Yeah, talk to that fool before his mouth get him into trouble!" Wild Blood added as they were leaving. Wild Blood was a cold-blooded gangster first. Everything else came after.

However, with Chandar, it was business, first. His biggest objective was making piles of legal money. As such, he wanted to give Willie Black a chance to be the next big star—everyone would benefit from it. Still, everything inside of the Big Homie was screaming that Willie Black was bad news. Dude had a fucked-up attitude. Chandar knew it was only a matter of time.

Willie Black would reveal himself to be a muthafuckin' problem.

CHAPTER FOURTEEN

Big Time's new connect supplied him with enough cocaine to transform him into a very powerful person on the streets of Jamaica Queens. The prices that the mysterious connect was able to charge for each kilo was unheard of in the New York region. It was almost as if the connect was giving the drugs away! Consequently, Big Time was responsible for feeding a lot of families. He was touching plenty of paper and the kid was showing plenty of love—you couldn't tell him he wasn't the mayor.

The passenger door of the dark cloud grey Chevy Tahoe was open and Big Time was leaning against the truck waiting for Kool-Aid to come outside. Jay-Z's voice poured from the bangin' system with clarity, and his lyrics had everyone in the vicinity in a zone.

'I spit that other shit, that's a nice muthafucka shit, Feds tryna follow me around—deep cover shit, nigga!'

Booga and the little niggaz on the corner hustling were singing along as they drank 40's of Olde English and served customers.

'You're beer money, I'm all year money/ I'm poppin' you don't gotta count it, it's all there money.'

Kool-Aid came out the house with a black hoodie on carrying a brown paper bag. He gave Big Time dap and passed him the bag of money.

"Damn nigga, you went and copped another truck?" Kool-Aid asked, walking around inspecting the Tahoe.

"Nah nigga, that shit ain't mine," Big Time said tossing the brown paper bag on the passenger seat.

"Oh." Kool-Aid scoped the block out while talking to Big Time. "Who's shit is that?"

Big Time dug in his pocket and pulled out the keys. "That joint right there is yours, Fam!" He announced and tossed the keys to Kool-Aid.

Kool-Aid caught the keys and fumbled with them before he was able to look back and forth from the truck to Big Time to see if this nigga was bullshitting.

"Get the fuck outta here, nigga! Stop playing."

"I ain't playing, Fam—that's you," Big Time said climbing into the passenger seat. "Come on, I need you to drop me off at my baby's mother house so I can get my car."

Kool-Aid didn't need to be told twice!

'When I see em in the streets, I don't see none of that—Damn playboy, where the fuck is the Hummer at?'

Kool-Aid was yelling along with the song as he jumped behind the wheel and pulled off.

"Ayo!" Big Time said, turning down the music. "The paperwork is in the glove compartment. I was gonna cop you the Yukon Denali but this joint had your name written all over it. You like it, Fam?"

"Hell yeah! What's that, a trick question? Where you get it from?"

"My people put me up on this federal auction that be jumping off the last Saturday of every month. You know me and you been doing this shit together from day one. I just wanted to show my 'preciation."

"No doubt, son! That was good fuckin' looking out—I love you for this shit!" Kool-Aid said from the heart.

After Kool-Aid dropped Big Time off next to his four-door Benz coupe, he followed Big Time to the apartment they had in Far Rockaway. Big Time wanted to put away the fifteen grand that Kool-Aid just gave him. Their hustle was going good and Big Time was content, but Kool-Aid was what some people would call scary. Truth be told, he had good reason to be scared. The money was coming in so quick that it was becoming harder and harder to hide. Plus, Big Time was flossing as if shit in the hood was sweet. Kool-Aid knew better! Cheddar would always breed jealousy, and it was just a matter of time before the wolves paid them a visit. That was one fear.

Another fear was the Feds. History taught that every individual or team that was fortunate enough to accumulate large sums of currency in the drug game always became unfortunate enough to either get killed or sentenced to football numbers by an ex-klan member in a black robe.

"This shit is crazy, Fam!" Big Time said removing bundles of cash from the safe. "On this next run we getting ten of them thangs. I don't want us to do no shopping or nothing until everything is gone, it shouldn't take more than thirty days. When we finish, I'm giving you a hundred grand."

That blew Kool-Aid's mind! A hundred gees? This shit was like a dream come true, but Kool-Aid still felt that he needed to confide in Big Time about his insecurities.

"Damn son! We did it! We the brick layers! I'm not even gonna lie son, I never imagined that we'd be doing it this big. I need you to feel me though," Kool-Aid said, getting serious. "We need to put together a security team or something. We can't be driving around with all this money like shit is sweet, we gotta find some niggaz that's gonna bang that steel.

We touching some major paper, son. We gonna have to protect it."

Big Time was nodding his head in agreement, "That's true. You right, Fam. I'm putting you in charge of that, so you can start putting a squad together now. Another thing, I'm about to start being more organized, we about to tighten up. Instead of me and you dealing with everybody individually, we're gonna start hitting one person at each spot and let that person deal with everybody else. For example, on 110th and Merrick, I'm just gonna hit Stan with a brick and tell him what to bring back. Anybody hustling on 110th will have to deal with him."

"On 112th we could hit Mike, and Booga could handle the Bully," Kool-Aid added with a hint of excitement.

Big Time and Kool-Aid was about to regulate the hood! As far as they were concerned they paid their dues, and now it was time to shine.

The first step Kool-Aid took to bring their plan to life was to recruit two gunmen. Trey was only seventeen, but he had been buggin' Big Time to put him on for months. The youngster wasn't bringing any experience to the table, but for a thousand dollars a week, Trey would push his mother's wig back if she violated. Kool-Aid gave him a black nine with two extra clips. Trey's assignment was to be Big Time's shadow. Wherever Big Time went, Trey was to be right there.

Trigger was a stick-up kid that just came home from serving five years in prison. Kool-Aid assigned him to help Stan out at the spot on 110th and Merrick, but Trigger's principal assignment was to be Kool-Aid's personal enforcer. When Kool-Aid barked, it would be Trigger that bit.

The next step was even more crucial. They had to transform Booga, Stan, and Mike into sure 'nuff bosses. Big Time supplied them with a brick a piece, and in an attempt at assuring loyalty, he went to the government auction and copped new whips for his three overnight draft picks.

Stan got the Black kitted out Yukon Denali. Mike's crazy ass came up with a silver Acura RL sedan. Booga was instantly catapulted to hood rich status when he came through pushing a burgundy drop-top 350Z!

Everything seemed to be coming together like butt cheeks.

But surely, anything worth its weight in gold is sure to be tested...

$$$

Reggie Ransom had been scheming on Big Time for over a week, but for some reason he wasn't able to catch up with ole' boy. He drove through 110th and Merrick, 112th and Guy R. Brewer, and he must've drove up and down Supthin Boulevard a hundred times. Not once did he spot the gold Mercedes Benz or Black Escalade that Big Time drove.

Nevertheless, Reggie Ransom wasn't one to easily give up. He and his protégé', Barrell, were in the back seat of 6A's Camry cruising down the Bully like predators in search of a particular prey. The Grim Reaper preferred hunting alone, but Barrell was a monster in the making. Even monsters needed to be groomed.

Up top, in some circles Barrell was known as Country because the truth was, he was a cold-blooded country boy straight out of Raleigh, North Carolina. He was known for bustin' his gun hard in the Walnut Terrace section of Raleigh. His rep was so strong that when two of his boys, Dre and Kap, were copping coke from a Dominican dude in the Washington Heights section of Manhattan, they enlisted Barrell to rob their connect. It was sweet so Dre and Kap were able to set it up immediately. Barrell ran through Poppi like a hot knife through butter and came up with three bricks of raw! They hauled ass back down to Raleigh where Dre and Kap were moving the coke, but Barrell was turned on to a new kind of high. Baby boy was eager to pull his next robbery!

Their second trip to the Big Apple was just as sweet as the first trip, and it wasn't long before Barrell realized that he was addicted to doing stick ups. With Barrell, it was the excitement and the mere possibility of grave consequences that made him look forward to pulling the next heist. It was sort of like flirting with death in exchange for enormous rewards.

One particular night, Kap called Barrell and told him that they needed to make an emergency trip to New York. They weren't supposed to go back up top for at least another two weeks but someone had stolen a brick and a half of coke from Kap, and Barrell was still thirsty for the thrill so he instantly agreed to go.

No sooner did Barrell hang up the phone from speaking with Kap, he heard someone knocking at the front door. When Barrell opened the door, he was surprised to see Dre standing there, fresh to death from head to toe, with a big ass smile on his face.

"You gone live a long time, I was just finna call you!" Barrell said as Dre came inside. "We finna take another trip to New York, I just got off the phone with Kap."

"Mane, fuck that nigga!" Dre said, surprising the hell out of Barrell.

Barrell knew that Dre and Kap didn't get along too well, but this was the first time he heard Dre display open disrespect. Kap used to be that nigga. He used to go crazy hard until he fucked up and got into a motorcycle accident that damn near killed him. He was fortunate to pull through, but his leg was messed up for life, so the doctors said, and that took a lot of fight out of him.

Nevertheless, Barrell still had respect for Kap. They were friends and that was the bottom line.

"You trippin'! Somebody stole' a brick and a half from that nigga. We finna make a move!" Barrell said anxious to do another robbery.

"Mane, I got that nigga shit! Fuck that nigga! You don't gotta go nowhere, I'm giving you half of what I took from that nigga."

Betrayal! Barrell felt as if Dre was putting him in a fucked-up position, and that shit wasn't cool at all. So Baby Boy had to put a straightening on it.

"Dre, I fucks with both of y'all. He my mane just like you my mane. I'm not finna be in the middle of that, for real."

"And I respect that," Dre said, giving Barrell some dap. "You sure you skraight? I can still break you off with something."

"Nah, I'm good."

So, in a sense, there *was* honor among thieves. Still, with Dre out of the picture, Barrell and Kap was a man short. They needed at least three people to pull off a job. It was times like this that Barrell wished his friend Rodney, A.K.A. Hot Rod, was still alive. Hot Rod was an official dude, but like so many young blacks, he was murdered before he had a chance to live.

Something inside Barrell told him that they were speeding, it might not have been a good time to take that trip. But greed overpowered him, and destiny pulled Barrell, Kap, and Corey to exactly where they were supposed to be.

Broadway and Amsterdam were the main two streets that ran through Washington Heights. Both streets were like an open market to anyone who wanted to purchase cocaine.

Kap would normally cop a few grams from one of the many peddlers in order to detect a weakness in their operation. Once the weakness was identified, the robbery was planned and then carried out.

The first robbery they ever did was on 140th Street and Broadway. A Dominican guy named Coochie kept his stash inside an old Ford Taurus that was parked down the hill from where he did business. Coochie's workers kept at least two kilos of cocaine stashed inside a building enabling them to sell ounces, big eighth's, and an occasional quarter key for hours without going to the main stash. When the supply got low, Coochie would send one of the workers to fetch two more kilos from the main stash in the car to bring back to the building.

After Kap peeped how it was going down, the robbery itself was a piece of cake. Barrell left Poppi handcuffed in the back seat of the Taurus butt naked, and they went back to Raleigh with three bricks. About a month later they hit Coochie's stupid ass again for close to eight bricks.

On 151st Street and Broadway, Flaco had an operation that proved to be a little more difficult to penetrate, or so he thought. As usual, Kap approached the worker and told him that he wanted to buy 14 grams of straight coke. The worker led him into a decrepit looking building and they went up to the second floor where Poppi quickly tapped on an apartment door. When the door was opened, Kap was surprised to see a youthful looking Latino kid brandishing what appeared to be an Uzi machine gun. Once they were inside the apartment, Kap was patted down and instructed to have a seat at the kitchen table which was the only piece of furniture inside the dilapidated dwelling. After counting and re-counting the $350, the worker left the apartment leaving Kap with the gun-toting kid, only to return minutes later with the 14 grams of coke.

It was easy to deduce that the stash was nearby.

Next, they sent Dre to the same worker to purchase an ounce of coke, but this time Barrell went inside the building first. When the worker led Dre to the apartment, Barrell was on the staircase between the second and third floors—plotting! They weren't in the apartment for five minutes before Poppi came out and went straight to the stash, which was inside the apartment right next door.

Bingo!

Barrell waited until Dre was gone, and he sat inside the building for a good twenty minutes before Poppi came back with his next customer. Barrell watched as they went inside the apartment. As soon as Poppi came back out to go to the stash, Barrell was on his heels.

"Easy Poppi," he said, sliding up from behind, letting the barrel of the bulldog .44 press against the side of Poppi's head. "Don't turn this into a homicide."

"Listen man, don't kill me. It ain't worth it," Poppi said in clear English.

"I'm gonna leave that up to you Amigo. How many people inside the apartment?"

"There's no one inside, I'm the only one with a key."

"Good! Open the door and move slow, all I want is the coke."

That was a lie! Poppi had close to six bricks of coke and a little over $10,000 in cash. Barrell put it all in a duffle bag that he found in a closet and left Poppi handcuffed to a radiator. And once again, they were hitting the highway.

For the emergency trip, they decided to hit Flaco's operation one more time. The logic was that Poppi wouldn't be expecting to get hit twice. Of course, this was the same logic they used when they robbed Coochie for the second time. Kap volunteered to be the feeler again and he went to buy an ounce of coke from the same worker. They went through the same routine as the first time, only this time they switched apartments. The apartment that was used for the transaction two weeks before was now the stash spot, and the stash spot was now the place where they were conducting transactions. Since Corey was the new face, everybody agreed that he would be the one to get the drop on Poppi. Barrell took one look at Corey and it was written all over shorty's face—he was scared to death! Nevertheless, it was time to man up.

When Corey went inside the building, Kap and Barrell watched from a safe distance as the worker stood outside waiting for his next customer. It didn't take long before someone came along and unknowingly followed the worker into the ambush. A transaction normally took less than ten minutes, fifteen minutes at the most. So, it was only natural for Kap and Barrell to begin to worry after thirty minutes passed and there was still no sign of Corey.

"Shit!" Barrell yelled, amping himself up. He was ready to go see what the fuck was up!

"Chill Mane, anything could've happened. Let's just wait it out," Kap said trying to think positive.

Then the worker came back out the building looking around nervously. That's when they knew that something was wrong.

"Fuck! I'm finna run up on this nigga!" Barrell said clutching the bull dog on his waist.

"Let me go first. I'm finna act like I'm tryna buy some more coke. If he let me inside you come right behind us."

"Bet!"

Barrell watched his man limp across the street dipping through traffic. Poppi looked like he was spooked when Kap approached him, but after a minute they headed toward the building. Barrell jetted across the street like a mad man. It was amazing he wasn't hit by a car. He made it inside the building before Kap and the worker made it to the second-floor landing. Barrell ran up the stairs two at a time and before Poppi could knock on the apartment door, Barrell had the drop on him.

Poppi recognized Barrell's face instantly. "My friend, you come back," the worker said with a bit of confidence.

"Where my mafuckin' people at? I ain't tryna hur that shit!" Barrell said, grabbing Poppi by the shirt and putting the .44 under his chin.

"Amigo, you shouldn't worry about your friend. It's your own safety that should concern you."

As if on cue, the door to the stash spot opened and a muscular Dominican guy was holding a gun to Corey's head. Two more Dominicans descended from the staircase, one was unarmed but the other one was carrying that formidable looking Uzi.

Kap spun around aiming his gun at the guy with the Uzi.

"Listen," Kap said trying to reason. "We just came for our friend. We don't want no trouble, mane."

The guy on the stairs that was unarmed said something in Spanish to his friend that Barrell was gripping by the shirt, and Poppi responded briefly.

"You," the unarmed man said looking at Barrell. "You have something that belongs to me, no? After it is returned, you can have your friend back."

Barrell knew that they guy was talking about the coke and the money that he took from them during the first robbery.

"Mane, that shit is gone," Barrell stated. "But dig this, we know we fucked up, Poppi. This shit right hur look real ugly. Let my people go and you get my word as a man, you won't ever see us around hur again."

The unarmed man smiled, a sinister smile. Dude was the fucking Boss! This was the guy who ran the entire operation. His name was Flaco.

"I'm afraid that's not going to happen..."

$$$

Reggie Ransom couldn't believe this shit! He spent days in an abandoned apartment that was right next door to one of the apartments that Poppi used to conduct business in. He was waiting on Poppi to receive the motherload so he could pull a two-eleven, but shit always found a way to go wrong.

First, this crack-head ass dude robbed Poppi at a time when the stash was probably on "E". That was bad enough because it put Flaco and his people on point and they raised their security level. Now, the motherload had finally arrived. The Grim Reaper knew because he was looking through the peephole when Flaco and two of his flunkies entered the apartment next door carrying numerous shopping bags weighted down. Reggie Ransom was just waiting for the right time to attack. He had his eye glued to the peephole, damn near ready to fall asleep after hours of surveillance when he witnessed this scary ass dude waving a gun at Poppi. The guy was so scared the gun was literally shaking in his hand. Out of nowhere, two Dominicans who must've been camped out somewhere in the building got the drop on ole' boy. They caught dumb-dumb slipping, and his dumb ass let them take his gun right out of his hand before they busted him over the head and dragged him inside the stash house.

186

Reggie Ransom was ready to abort the mission, but he decided to be patient. Too much money was at stake! He put his ear to the wall and tried to hear what was going on in the apartment next door, but he couldn't hear anything. Almost a half an hour had passed when he heard noise coming from the hallway and ran to the peephole. The Grim Reaper couldn't believe his eyes. The crackhead was back, the same one from the first robbery. He and one of his comrades had poppi hemmed up at gun point.

Reggie Ransom jetted to the kitchen sink and splashed some water on his face. His eyes were burning! When he made it back to the peephole it was almost as if he was watching an old gangster flick. Playing out before his eyes was a Mexican stand-off; guns were drawn and fingers were on triggers.

The Grim Reaper was exhausted, but he knew he needed to do something and he needed to do it now! It was get rich or die trying.

He pulled out his chrome Desert Eagle, chambered a live round, then slowly opened the front door. The apartment Reggie Ransom crept from allowed him to ease up from the blind side of the two Dominicans by the staircase. When they heard the door squeaking open, Flaco turned around just in time to see Reggie Ransom walking toward him. By the time Flaco saw the gun it was too late! Reggie Ransom grabbed his skinny ass in a yoke and jammed the Eagle into his temple.

"Road dawg, listen to me and listen to me closely," Reggie Ransom hissed at the man holding the Uzi. "Put your gun down and you live to see another day. I promise you, this is just a robbery—it's nothing personal."

"You'll never make it out of the building alive. My people are all over the place," Flaco boasted, attempting to infuse fear into the situation.

"A gun in your face and that's all you can come up with?" Reggie Ransom quipped. "Listen, life is short Flaco. You got ten seconds to tell your people to drop their guns. After that I'm putting your brains all over this wall...ten...nine...eight..."

The guy with the Uzi aimed his gun at Reggie Ransom.

"Seven...six...five..."

Barrell cocked the hammer back on the bulldog! Shit was about to get ugly.

"Four...three—"

"Put the fucking guns down!" Flaco shouted.

The guy with the Uzi looked around as if he was confused. Reggie Ransom could see the sweat trickling down his cheek, but ole' boy was reluctant to drop the gun.

"Just put the gun down Joselito, it's okay," Flaco relented in defeat. He was the boss, and he knew that no amount of money or drugs was worth dying for, so he submitted.

Joselito slowly placed the Uzi on the floor. Kap spun around and turned his gun on the guy inside the apartment.

"You too Poppi, put your gun down," Kap said with a smile.

"Freddy, put the gun down," Flaco called out. As soon as Freddy put his gun down, Corey jetted out of the apartment and into the hallway looking around nervously.

"Young Buc, get the guns," Reggie Ransom said kicking the Uzi toward Corey. "And while you're at it, get the drugs too—hurry up!"

Kap forced the guy named Freddy to lay down on the floor in the apartment. Then they brought the other three Dominicans inside and made them do the same thing.

The three weighted down shopping bags contained six kilos of cocaine in each bag, but two bricks were missing from one of the bags.

"Since I had to clean up the mess y'all made I'm taking two of these bags," Reggie Ransom demanded. With his hand near his weapon, he studied their faces to see if that was a problem.

"Oh hell nah, mane!" Kap barked.

"Let him take two," Barrell surrendered, respecting the old head's gangsta.

"Mane, we gotta split three ways," Kap pleaded.

"So what! We wouldn't be splitting nothing if old head didn't hold us down!" Barrell said with finality.

And before anyone could stop him, Barrell stood over the Dominicans and let his bulldog bark. The game was over!

This was how Reggie Ransom met Barrell, A.K.A. Country!

Now Reggie Ransom instructed 6A to pull behind a grey Tahoe that was idling on 116th Avenue with its hazard lights blinking on and off. Kool-Aid was standing on the sidewalk talking on his cell phone.

"There that nigga go right there!" The Grim Reaper whispered, pointing at Kool-Aid. He was thinking aloud but Barrell was already amped up, and as they exited the vehicle Reggie Ransom noticed his protégé reaching for the toast tucked in his waist.

"Be easy, Road dawg. The young boy aiight, I don't wanna spook 'em," Reggie Ransom said, as he quickly surveyed the terrain. "Jet up in the store and grab us some candy and stuff. Take your time. I got this."

$$$

When Kool-Aid peeped the burgundy Toyota Camry pull up behind his truck, he instinctively turned his attention to the entrance of the store and wondered what was taking Trigger so long.

Trigger was getting paid a gee a week to watch Kool-Aid's back, but as far as Kool-Aid was concerned he could've saved a gee and watched his own motherfucking back. This nigga Trigger was slipping! As Kool-Aid was putting his mack down on

191

the phone, he noticed Reggie Ransom and another dude getting out of the Camry.

"Damn!" Kool-Aid muttered aloud.

He knew he and Reggie Ransom wasn't beefing, but he could've sworn he peeped the other kid adjusting something on his waist before he went inside the store. Kool-Aid ended his phone call as the Grim Reaper approached him.

"O.G., what's good with you?" Kool-Aid asked, trying to feel a nigga out.

"Everything is lovely, Killer!" Reggie Ransom responded, acknowledging the fact that Kool-Aid had a confirmed murder under his belt.

"Oh yeah?" Kool-Aid said with a smile. "The way your man just came through I almost thought niggaz was trying to intimidate me or something."

"Nah Road dawg! You my guy, I fucks with you for real. The young boy is just like you. He's in training, and you know me, I train 'em to go!"

Reggie Ransom glanced at the Tahoe and continued, "Who's truck is this? Niggaz doing it real big around here, huh?"

"That be me O.G., you like it?" Kool-Aid was one of the few people who was actually comfortable around the Grim Reaper, and Reggie Ransom appreciated it because even a monster hated always being treated like a monster.

"Road dawg, you doing the damn thing, and don't let nobody tell you no different, ya heard?"

"I heard!" Kool-Aid said.

Just then, Trigger came out of the store. When he recognized the Grim Reaper's face he immediately pulled out his .357 long.

"Kool-Aid, what's good?" Trigger asked, gripping the huge revolver tightly.

Before Kool-Aid could respond, Reggie Ransom snapped!

"Nigga is you crazy? You pulling out a gun on me?"

"Don't start no trouble it won't be no trouble O.G.!" Trigger said, looking as if he was about to have a panic attack.

"Nigga, I'll make you eat that muthafuckin' gun!" Reggie Ransom said walking toward Trigger.

Trigger started backing up, reaching behind him for the door handle so he could go back in the store. "Chill O.G., I told you we don't want no trouble," he pleaded.

193

"You know the rules, don't pull no gun out if you ain't gonna use it—shoot me, nigga!"

Before Reggie Ransom could reach Trigger, his scared ass had already ran back into the store.

"This shit is crazy! That nigga' with you?" Reggie Ransom asked looking back at Kool-Aid.

Kool-Aid just shook his head with disappointment. "Not no more," he decided. "His faggot ass just got tested, and he failed miserably."

As Barrell came out of the store, an idea popped into Reggie Ransom's head. "Road dawg, if you need somebody to hold you down, I got the perfect person," he proposed to Kool-Aid. He ushered Barrell over to them and made the introductions.

"Country, I want you to meet Kool-Aid, he official with a capitol "O". And Kool-Aid, this is my protégé, Barrell A.K.A Country. He's looking for work, and I promise you, he ain't gonna run! He's gonna bust that gun at an all-time high. I put my stamp on that."

Kool-Aid looked Barrell over, nodding his head in approval. He was feeling everything the Grim Reaper was saying.

"What y'all niggaz doing right now?" He asked, looking from Reggie Ransom to Barrell.

"Shit, we doing whatever you tryna do," Barrell replied going with the flow. He was always eager to make his mark.

"Aiight bet, come on let's go for a ride. I got a few stops to make."

Reggie Ransom paid 6A his fare and they jumped in Kool-Aid's truck.

After the Tahoe pulled off, Trigger peeped his head out of the store to see if the coast was clear. Despite the fact he had bitched up on the spot, he amped himself up as he stepped back out on the block.

"That nigga lucky he left," he said to himself. "I was about to air his ass out."

CHAPTER FIFTEEN

It was Rosso Corsa Red.

Wild Blood had just copped the Ferrari F360 Spider, and the guy at the dealership was adamant about the actual color of the car's exterior.

"It's not candy-apple red, it's not fire engine red. This car is Rosso Corsa red. *Rosso Corsa* red. Remember that!"

Wild Blood couldn't care less what the guy wanted to call it. All he was concerned with was driving one of them bad boys off the lot.

The exotic vehicle had a peanut-butter colored interior and bucket racing seats.

Chandar felt as if he was having an out of body experience as he watched the manager at Exotic Motor Cars pass Wild Blood the keys to the brand-new Ferrari. A staff member quickly slapped a temporary tag on the back of the car, and the joy in Wild Blood's eyes filled Chandar with pride. The home team had come a long way. Gone were the days when they had to hug the block to make a dollar. Gone were the days when they had to result to murder in order to protect the currency they made from the block.

Chandar smiled as Wild Blood drove the Rosso Corsa red Ferrari off the lot, it's engine purring.

"Now that fool look like the president of Loud Mouth Records," Chandar thought as he ran and jumped behind the wheel of his White Porsche Cayenne Turbo.

The two vehicles raced through the streets of New York making it clear that the Cayenne was no match for the F360.

They made it to the Soul Convention in record time. After they double-parked, Wild Blood inspected his newest acquisition as if it were a baby.

"Ayo! This shit is crazy low, you don't think I should get it raised up a little? I fuck around and hit a pot hole and it's a wrap."

"Stop tripping, fool! If you tear it up, cop another one. That's how that shit go," Chandar boasted. "That joint is supposed to be low, that's how she giddy up!"

Wild Blood digested the logic of the ghetto star's statement, and then without warming, he gave Chandar a big ass hug.

"You hear me, Big Homie? Without you none of this shit was possible. Word to Blood, I ain't gonna let you down!" Wild Blood pledged. Right then and there he resolved to make Loud Mouth Records a huge success.

"Don't let yourself down, Playboy," Chandar shot back as they walked inside the Soul Convention.

$$\$$$

When Chandar and Wild Blood walked inside the studio it was a full house. Willie Black and Cub was up in the spot eager to get their project off the ground. Maxwell Smart was playing around with the mixing board while Vinnie Garrett fed him instructions. Lucky was sitting on a stool in front of a microphone with headphones propped up on his head, and Reggie Ransom and Barrell was posted up in the back of the room observing everything. Jeff White had migrated back to the West coast to assume his position as C.E.O. of Colossal Publishing so he was out of the picture.

Chandar approached Reggie Ransom and they spoke briefly before the Grim Reaper called Barrell over and introduced him to the ghetto star. Chandar automatically accepted Barrell as family on the strength of Reggie Ransom.

Chandar was actually happy that the ole' head finally decided to check in, and he knew he needed to find something for the O.G. to do before he got restless.

While they were laying in the cut kicking it, Chandar overheard Willie Black beefing with Vinnie. Dude was getting loud and being disrespectful.

"I'm saying, we wasting time! Makavelli could do whatever he tryna do when we get finish with our session," Willie Black barked as if he had a valid point.

"Chill Fam!" Vinnie said trying to get ole' boy to lower his voice.

The truth was, Vinnie Garrett was pushing to make the 4-1-0 Hustlers a priority. He had managed Willie Black and Cub for over three years and felt that the time for the 4-1-0 Hustlers to shine was way overdue. Still, he needed Willie Black to be patient. Wild Blood was the boss and that was the bottom line. Unfortunately, the boss wanted Makavelli's mixtapes to be top priority so that's what they were working on.

"What's the problem, Playboy?" Chandar asked. He was looking from Willie Black to Vinnie, but his question was clearly directed at Willie Black.

Willie Black sighed, expelling air like a tire catching a flat. "Real talk, I don't got no problem. But I'm saying, my record been on the back burner forever. Loud Mouth just signed a distribution deal with Def Jam and we in here working on a mixtape?

That shit don't make no sense. I'm saying, I just want out of my contract."

Chandar was tired of this nigga's bullshit! He looked at Cub. "And you feel the same way?"

Cub nodded his head up and down, and Vinnie Garrett shook his head in disbelief.

Chandar thought for a second and then said, "It's done. Your contract is void. I'm sorry we couldn't do business together and I wish y'all the best."

And that was it. The 4-1-0 Hustlers were no longer a part of Loud Mouth. They were gone. Finished! *Finito!*

Nevertheless, Chandar wasn't stunting that because they still had a promising R&B act, and besides that, the ghetto star had confidence that Wild Blood would do what needed to be done to make sure everything turned out right.

It just so happened that everyone was in for a huge surprise! The next best thing was right there under their noses, ready to carry Loud Mouth to the next level. He was already sitting on a stool with headphones over his ears.

"Ayo Chandar!" Makavelli's voice came through the speakers. Everybody in the studio turned to look at Makavelli at the same time, as if they just remembered he was there. The homie just bobbed his head up and down as if he was comfortable in the spotlight.

"Ayo! Fuck all that sucka shit, it's about to go down for real, ya heard? I'm about to do what I do. Me and Maxwell put this throwback joint together, this the joint we gonna use to start my mixtape. Remember that KRS-One joint?" Makavelli started singing. "Boogie down productions, ductions...will always get paid, paid..."

Everybody started singing along, "We take the wackest songs, and make them betttter..."

"Aight, hold up, hold up, I just wanted to make sure we was on the same page. This how we doing the throwback, and you know we gonna have to send a crazy shot out to Kris; he killed it with this joint. Max, you ready?"

Maxwell Smart nodded his head giving Makavelli the green light.

"Aiight, check it...Loud Mouth Records, records...Will always stay paid, paid... we drive Mercedes Benz, and cock 380 twins, twins...so, remember, who brought it back to the hood, hood... We're up to no good, good our guns be..."

Max brought the track in! "Bustin', Bustin, Bustin'—Pow!"

And Makavelli started spitting that fire!

"The governments loving this predicament they got us in/ it's evident/ Blood residents/ get dead presidents/

They're watching us/ clocking through the Infra-red binoculars/ visions of the million-man march, it's the apocalypse/

Flip the script, read 'the Prince'—I'm talking on my celly/ if Tupac's alive he's the real Makavelli/

No more Niccolo/ on no!/ pass the E&J and cola/ I'll leave you shaking like a Motorola—"

And that's how it began...

In a matter of weeks, Makavelli's mixtape saturated the streets. He performed at local clubs, and damn near every other vehicle driving through the five boroughs was bangin' his shit. The homie was single-handedly holding it down on the rap tip, and he was already creating a buzz in the North East region. The streets were speculating that Makavelli might be the one to bring the East back!

Nevertheless, wherever there is success, you're sure to find envy! So, it didn't come as a surprise that there was a healthy dose of hate to accompany the love that Makavelli was receiving.

The haters began saying that Makavelli was disrespecting the late Tupac Shakur by using the slain rapper's alias.

If that wasn't bad enough, Willie Black was back on the scene, and he dropped a mixtape called *Warning Shots* that had the city going crazy!

True to form, the streets began instigating immediately. Everyone speculated that *Warning Shots* was aimed at Loud Mouth Records.

On the title track, *Hustla 'Til I Die*, Willie Black rapped over the instrumental of *Ambitionz Az A Ridah* off of Tupac's double CD: *All Eyez on Me.*

Willie Black spit:

"I'm a muthafuckin' boss/ wrong nigga to cross/ I could get ya body lost/ somewhere down in the gulf/

I could get ya head hit by a nigga up north/ Couple of dollars, will have you in the truck of the Impala/ Holla!

When you see me, I got work for days/ from half O's to kilos, smoking purple haze/

I got black tar diesel/ consignment for my people/ I'm a fuckin hustler. Willie Black gon' feed you!/

Pussy nigga see through, I keep my eyes on 'im/ if a nigga too slick, gotta sic my spies on 'im/ put thick thighs on 'im with some phat ass lips/ lil' momma down to ride, plus she phat as shit/

*I'll let shawty put in work, in a Prada skirt/ have ya
body cold and stiff inside the church/ can't recognize the
body riding inside the hearse/*

*It's gonna be some lonely nights inside the dirt/ first
nigga act up, first nigga get merked/ Got killers on my
side and they putting in work/*

*I'm the muthafuckin Boss! Warning Shots nigga/ Y'all
some funny niggaz"*

Willie Black was laughing all over the track and flowing at the same time as he threw shots at anyone who ever tried to hold him back. His entire mixtape was a spectrum of raw talent, and it was just a matter of time before the right people would take notice and give the 4-1-0 Hustlers a deal.

CHAPTER SIXTEEN

Makavelli was pulling all-nighters in the studio, working extra hard to stay on top of the game. His name was ringing bells up and down the East Coast and he was slowly but surely earning the respect of his peers in the music industry. However, Willie Black was like a thorn in his side.

Everybody knew about the 4-1-0 Hustlers being dropped from Loud Mouth, and even though it was being done indirectly, everybody knew that Willie Black was throwing rocks at the throne. It was bad blood and that was the bottom line.

Makavelli listened to the song called, *Y'all Some Funny Niggaz* one more time. He analyzed Willie Black's flow, bar for bar, listening to his nemesis laughing over the track. Makavelli knew exactly what needed to be done. Willie Black was a problem, and as such, Willie Black needed to be shut down!

Maxwell Smart played a variety of tracks for Makavelli, digging deep and offering some of his most exclusive beats. Makavelli closed his eyes and listened to each beat intently as if his life depended on his choosing the right beat. When he heard it, he knew it was the one. He jumped up excitedly.

"That's it! That's that muthafucka right there. Max, you a beast!"

Makavelli listened to the beat for a good twenty minutes before he was ready to lay down his vocals.

After they put it all together, Max called Vinnie Garrett and told him to stop by the studio. As soon as Vinnie walked in and heard the hook, he knew it was on! This one song was either going to take Makavelli over the top, or it was going to be the beginning of the demise of his short-lived career. The homie was openly challenging Willie Black by responding to, *Y'all Some Funny Niggaz.*

All bias aside, Vinnie had to admit, Makavelli's response was straight fire!

"Damn son, that hook is bananas! It's perfect for that beat. Where you get this beat from? Let me hear that shit again, take it from the top."

Maxwell Smart smiled while he worked the mixing board. He gave Makavelli a high five as the track invaded the studio again. The track began with an excerpt from Willie Black's song. Max had looped Willie Black laughing and let it play a few times.

"Ha,Ha,Ha,Ha,Ha,/ Ha,ha,ha,ha,ha..."

While Willie Black was laughing in the background, Makavelli was asking rhetorical questions. *"This nigga think shit funny? What am I, a fucking comedian?! What the fuck is this nigga laughing at? Check mate, dummy!"*

That's when Max dropped that hard ass beat and Makavelli just spazzed out on the track!

"AHHHH!!!"

"Laugh now cry later—the same thing that make you laugh will come back and haunt ya ass!

Laugh now cry later—and let it be known, they won't laugh when the homie Jerry Moore come home!

Laugh now cry later – hide the safe, think about plastic surgery and hide ya face!

Laugh now cry later—the same thing that make you laugh will come back and haunt ya ass!

I'm not a bit intimidated by ya little success/ you sold a thousand mixtapes, why your crew still stressed?/

You got dropped from the label, now you wearing a dress/ you're like food on the table you're about to get blessed/

With sixteen bars/ my hollow tip flow, will blow through the system of sixteen cars/ the chrome 40 cal. Will leave sixteen scars/ now you can laugh at that nigga, hardy har har har..."

Laugh Now Cry Later was exactly what the streets had anticipated! The world loves drama, and consequently, Makavelli's mixtape was selling like crack cocaine.

However, when Chandar heard *Laugh Now Cry Later* he wasn't enthused at all. Some people may have misinterpreted Chandar's disappointment as proof that the ghetto star was getting soft. But, the real deal was that Chandar knew the ramifications of beef. In the end, it was never worth it. Besides that, Chandar didn't need, nor did he want attention. His goal was to make an honest buck and strive to open as many doors as possible for his people.

Had Chandar known beforehand what Makavelli was up to, he would've never given the green light. But it was already done, and Chandar knew that every action caused a reaction, so once again Makavelli had the ghetto star in a situation.

Anticipating the worst, once again Chandar's focus was damage control.

CHAPTER SEVENTEEN

Jerry Moore felt as if he was in the middle of a nasty nightmare. He was coming from a visit with his attorney, Kevin Cohen, and now more than ever it seemed like the cards were stacked against him. Not only did he learn that his so-called Boo, his trusted ride or die chick, Denise, was cooperating with the government, but his overpriced mouth piece in an Armani suit was trying to get the Big Homie to switch sides. Jerry Moore was furious! Kevin Cohen had given him what was called 3500 material; grand jury minutes and other evidence that would be used at trial. Although Jerry Moore was ready to get it over with, he had to admit he wasn't prepared to start trial just yet. So, Mr. Cohen threw some bullshit in the air...

"Well Jerry, you can always consider the plea agreement. I don't think the code of the street that you adhere to will impress a jury much, but either way, it's your call. You're the one who has to live with decisions you make."

Jerry Moore looked at the lawyer with pure disdain. All the money his fat ass was getting paid to create a solid defense and his faggot ass was suggesting that they bow down?

"Shit, you can't change a player's game in the 9th inning," Jerry Moore told himself as he got off the elevator on the sixth floor.

"Voire Dire will begin next month..." Was the last thing Jerry Moore heard Mr. Cohen say before the visit was over. Everything else was incoherent. *Voire Dire* was the term used for jury selection.

The Big Homie had less than 45 days to prepare for trial.

$$$

When Jerry Moore rolled himself into the unit the first thing he noticed was Shan Will praying with a group of Muslims. They were in the T.V. room standing in rows with their hands folded over their chests and their heads bowed.

The Big Homie was already in a foul mood so this just pissed him off even more.

"All that shit this fool was talking about loving the Bible and now he wanna be Muslim?" Jerry Moore thought as he rolled his wheelchair to his room.

The Big Homie slammed his locker open and grabbed his phone book so he could go call A-Blood and tell him about the lawyer visit. When A-Blood answered his cell, Jerry Moore began to vent, telling the homie about Denise flipping and the possibility of starting trial next month. He expressed to A-Blood that he was no longer comfortable with Kevin Cohen representing him because of the suggestion Mr.

THE STAR IN THE MIRROR

Cohen made that they consider taking the plea agreement.

Surprisingly, A-Blood defended the lawyer's position, reminding Jerry Moore that by law Mr. Cohen had to at least put the government's offer on the table. Nevertheless, as a safety precaution, A-Blood volunteered to hire another attorney to assist Mr. Cohen and assure that the Big Homie received the best representation possible.

When Jerry Moore got off the phone with A-Blood he felt 85% better. The love and support he had on the outside was a blessing. Still, something that A-Blood said before the phone had cut off bothered the Big Homie. Jerry Moore rewound the conversation in his mind.

"You hear me, fool?" A-Blood had said with regret in his voice. "Me and Chandar jive beefing. For real, for real. I ain't beefing with him—I don't got nothing but love for the homie, but right now we're not seeing eye to eye."

Jerry Moore was stuck! After all they've been through, he couldn't fathom what A-Blood and Chandar could possibly be beefing about.

"Monkey bars, fool!" Jerry Moore said, using an outdated code that meant stop playing.

"You know I wouldn't bullshit about nothing like that. Word to Blood, I seen the homie last week after he signed the contracts for Loud Mouth. He literally bumped into me, and when I turned around and he saw it was me, he didn't even say excuse me, he just kept it moving. You already know."

Then the phone had cut off! Something definitely wasn't right! Jerry Moore didn't have a clue what they were tripping about but what he did know was that he needed to call Chandar to straighten it out.

A-Blood was family! He was the one who brought them home, made them take an oath so they could become Blood. He was also the one that gave Chandar the Authority to start his own set. Truth be told, A-Blood was the Big Homie for real!

Shan Will put his hand on Jerry Moore's shoulder breaking his chain of thought.

"What's poppin', Big Homie?"

Jerry Moore acknowledged the little homie but maintained a poker face. "We about to start trial next month," Jerry Moore said as he flipped through his phone book.

"Word?" Shan Will said. "I have to wait after four o' clock so I can put money on the phone and call my lawyer.

"You should've did that last night."

Shan Will caught that the Big Homie was in a sour mood so he didn't respond.

"I see you in there bumping your head with them hot ass niggaz! What happened to all that shit you was telling me about the Bible?" Jerry Moore continued in a confrontational tone.

"I told you that I always read the Bible, and I do. But I'm a Muslim. I was Muslim for years, I just wasn't practicing."

"If you're a Muslim then why you be reading the Bible? Don't y'all have your own book?"

"I read the Bible for studying purposes. Muslims believe that the Holy Qu'ran is the literal speech of God, and a lot of the stories in the Qu'ran are similar to those in the Bible. That's because, in order to be a Muslim, we have to believe in all of the Prophets, including Adam, Noah, Abraham, Moses and Jesus. And we have to believe in the books they brought. Moses brought the Torah, or the law, and Jesus brought the Injeel, or the Gospel. May the Peace and Blessings of Allah be on all of the Prophets. The only problem is that man mixed, diluted, and tampered with the Bible, so it's no longer pure."

213

Jerry Moore was humbled by the extent of Shan Will's knowledge, and he appreciated the wisdom the little homie used in his presentation. Shan Will wasn't being arrogant, nor was he being dogmatic. Shan Will reminded the Big Homie of Yahya Ruhani. Yahya was the leader of the Muslims at United States Penitentiary, Canaan. Jerry Moore used to go to services on Friday to hear the brother speak. After services, Jerry Moore would stay behind to ask questions and try to discredit Islam, but to his surprise, the Muslim religion made a lot of sense. Only because the Big Homie still wanted to make his own rules and basically do what he wanted to do, he didn't embrace the religion. Now, as he listened to Shan Will, he recognized that the Islamic way of life was worthy of further investigation.

"You really know your stuff, huh?" Jerry Moore said, lightening up on the little homie. "You're gonna have to tell me more about the Qu'ran later on, but for now, roll me to my room so we can go over some of this legal work I got."

$$\$\$\$$$

While Shan Will was reading over the 3500 material, Jerry got sidetracked and picked up one of his photo albums that sat atop the small metal desk in his cell. He began flipping through the pages and was immediately overcome by nostalgia. He had pictures of him and Lashawn snorkeling in the Bahamas and skydiving in Aruba. It may not have been worth the consequences, but the picture told a story that Jerry Moore had lived a good life...if only momentarily. There were pictures of him, Chandar, Infra-red, Wild Blood, Pop Dogg, Minnesota Fats, and A-Blood at Club Arizona in Brooklyn. Jerry Moore smiled as he came across a bunch of flicks taken at his welcome home party that A-Blood threw for him at Travagar Square. There was one picture in particular that held sentimental value to the Big Homie. It was a reflection of him and Don Chi Chi with a host of bad ass bitches. Sometimes it was still hard to believe that Don Chi Chi was gone. The little homie was a true G, and Jerry Moore missed him as if he was a blood relative.

"Ayo! Shan Will, check out this flick," Jerry Moore said, holding the photo album up.

Shan Will took his nose out of the legal work he was reading and came and stood next to the Big Homie.

"Drama! Who's that? A-Blood?"

Jerry Moore was smiling. "Yeah-yeah! That fool is a beast on them bikes!"

They were looking at a photo of A-Blood on a KX125 riding down the middle of the street with the bike's front tire up in the air at twelve o' clock! A little girl on the side walk was pointing at him. A few people sitting on milk crates stopped what they were doing to watch, and a guy and his dog observed in awe as A-Blood wheelied down 8th Avenue!

"This flick is a classic!" Jerry Moore noted as he reflected on all the good times he had with A-Blood bouncing through the five burroughs on their crotch rockets.

Just then, an Italian guy named Carmine tapped on the door before walking inside the cell. He left the door wide open and smiled at Jerry Moore sheepishly as he said, "Sorry to disturb you guys, but there's someone here to see the Big Homie."

Without warning, Jerry Moore received the shock of his life when that somebody stood in the door way of the cell.

"What? An old friend can't drop by and say hello?" The stranger asked as he noticed the surprised expression on Jerry Moore's face.

Standing in front of the Big Homie's cell on I-63 in MDC Brooklyn, wearing a prison Khaki uniform, was one of the most powerful underworld crime figures in America. To Jerry Moore, the mafia Boss was merely a good friend.

The Big Homie smiled and rolled out the red carpet, giving a warm welcome to none other than Anthony Orena!

CHAPTER EIGHTEEN

Chandar and Karen were lounging on the couch eating buttery popcorn while they watched the movie, *Bone Collector* starring Denzel Washington on DVD. Earlier in the evening Karen had whipped Chandar's ass in a game of scrabble, and the deal was that the loser had to prepare dinner. The truth was, the ghetto star enjoyed cooking. He chopped up some onions, bell peppers, fresh garlic and broccoli, and stir fried it all together in some olive oil. Simultaneously, he seasoned up and flame broiled a few Sirloin Streaks and made a side dish of wild rice with Cashews. It was a simple meal, but it was one that Karen enjoyed immensely.

Even after a long day at work Chandar didn't mind catering to Karen. She was in her last trimester of pregnancy and Chandar eagerly awaited for her to give birth to his little man. After the sonogram revealed that Karen was carrying a boy, Chandar celebrated! Finally, there would be someone to uphold the legacy! An heir to the throne. This is something that Chandar looked forward to.

The ghetto star had a complete background check done on Charles Watlington and learned that ole' boy was a full partner at a reputable law firm; The offices of Jacobi and Watlington. He set up a meeting with Charles and they put their minds together in an attempt to categorically analyze Chandar's financial situation. At the end of the day

Charles Watlington had set up four irrevocable business Trusts to meet Chandar's needs.

One Trust held Chandar's Edward Jones and GE Capital accounts in which he had over 1.7 million dollars invested. The beneficiary of that Trust was Chandar's daughter, Jasmine.

Another Trust held all of Chandar's major assets including his house in California and the home he shared with Karen in Long Island, New York. Also, every vehicle in his name was sold to the Trust. Karen was the beneficiary, and they agreed that their son would be added after he was born.

The third Trust held five CD's (cash deposits) totaling $25,000 before maturity. There was also a savings and checking account with Bank of America that held close to $20,000 that was placed in the Trust. Chandar thought long and hard, and after weighing and balancing, he made Jerry Moore the beneficiary of that Trust.

The final Trust held Chandar's share of Loud Mouth Records. Without thinking twice, he made his mother and his sister Pauline the beneficiaries of that Trust. Charles Watlington and Chandar's mother were the only ones with access to the accounts, aside from Chandar whom they elected as the general manager. Chandar had the power to regulate his money as he normally would, except now his taxes were minimized drastically and he had nothing for them to take. On paper the ghetto star was about a dollar away from being bankrupt, but as general manager of the Trusts, he was able to continue to live the lifestyle of the rich and famous.

Chandar also had over three million dollars in cash that he had stashed here and there for emergency purposes. After hitting a few of his safe deposit boxes and emptying two of his safes, he gave Charles Watlington three million dollars to deposit in an offshore bank account. Mr. Watlington had clout with the president of Bank Muzuho in the Bahamas. He claimed he did 'things like this' all the time, so opening an account with three million dollars in cash was a small thing.

When the movie was over, Karen leaned back on the couch and put her feet in Chandar's lap stealing him away from his thoughts.

"Baby Denzel did his thing. You know that's my man crush."

"He did aiight."

"Don't be hating on my boy! Baby, that movie was good."

"I said it was aiight," Chandar repeated, sticking to his guns with his answer.

Just then they were interrupted by Chandar's phone ringing. He looked at the screen and held up a hand.

"Give me a minute Boo, I think this is Jerry Moore."

After listening to the automated recording, Chandar pressed 5 to receive the call.

While the ghetto star spoke on the phone, Karen watched him as she contemplated the conversation they just had. As far as she was concerned, Chandar was her soul mate. He was a genuinely good person who always kept it real with her. He promised to love her forever and a day, and that's all Karen really wanted. A partner! Someone to love her and be there for her even when she had made mistakes. She wanted someone she could keep it real with, and deep down in her heart she believed Chandar was that person. So, when he got off the phone, she sought to bare her truth.

"Baby, do you really love me?"

Chandar looked at her with an easy smile but Karen wore a solemn expression on her face.

"You know I do, Boo...Always!"

"And you know I'm not perfect...I'm human." Karen's voice trembled slightly and Chandar could sense she was getting emotional. She continued, "I love you Chandar...I worship the ground you walk on and I always want us to be together. I don't want to lose you."

"And you're not gonna lose me, Boo," Chandar said, taking both of Karen's hands inside his.

"That's easy to say!" Karen cried, and that's when the storm broke through. She broke all the way down and began sobbing.

Chandar knew Karen had something on her mind but he didn't know what it could be. Then there was the possibility that she was just emotional as a result of her pregnancy. The ghetto star took his future wife in his arms and tried to comfort her. Karen was crying uncontrollably, but today she was determined to come clean, and after today there would be no more secrets.

"Whatever! You hungry?"

"Nah I'm good, and I know your fat ass ain't hungry 'cause we just ate."

"What???"

"I'm just fucking with you. Look at you getting all serious, you know I love your fat ass!" Chandar said, kissing the bottom of her feet.

"It's because of you that I'm fat, and it's not funny!" Karen said pouting.

"Let me ask you a question, Boo," Chandar said, looking deep into Karen's eyes. "Keep it real, if I was in an accident and lost both of my legs, would you still be with me? Think before you answer!"

"I don't have to think about that! Of course, I would still be with you—you're my man and I love you. Why wouldn't I still be with you?"

Chandar ignored her question, "What if I got locked up and sentenced to 25 years to life—would you hold me down?"

"Baby, you a trip. Let me find out you got me fucked up! If I'm riding with you. I'm gonna ride no matter what—bottom line! It don't matter what the circumstances are as long as you ain't trying to play me. You're asking me all these hypothetical questions. If you found out I used to be an exotic dancer before I got with you, would you still be with me?"

"Was you?"

"See, that's what I'm talking about. Answer the question, you started this shit!"

"If you was stripping when I met you, and I knew about it, nine times out of ten we wouldn't be together because I wasn't checking for a chick that shook her ass for a living. But if I was to find out right now that you used to strip, of course I would still be with you. For one, you ain't stripping no more, and for two, I already fell in love. Plus, you got that bomb ass head."

Karen punched him in the arm hard, but she was definitely satisfied with his answer.

"I Don't. Ever. Want to keep nothing from you," she swore.

"I know Boo, I feel the same way."

"If you...be mad at me..." Karen bent over clutching her stomach. "Ooh! Chandar, my stomach!"

"Baby, what's wrong? Talk to me!"

"I...I think it's time...Chandar! The baby is coming!"

Chandar damn near had a panic attack! He grabbed his cell phone and pressed 911!

"Take deep breaths, Boo!" He said trying to remember what he learned in all them boring classes he attended with Karen.

"911 emergency," the operator said.

"Yeah! My girl is about to have a baby!" Chandar yelled into the phone.

"Baby...who you talking to?" Karen asked in an aggravated tone.

"911."

Karen almost looked amused, "Boy, hang that phone up and come help me."

Chandar was irresolute, but he did as he was told.

"Grab the Prada bag out the hallway closet...it already got...everything I need...inside...you have to take me to the hospital... my water broke."

Chandar helped Karen clean herself up as best he could before ushering her to the Benz. Karen was timing her contractions and concluded that they were at least three minutes apart.

While they were driving. Chandar called his mother and sister, and he also called Karen's sister Regina. He told everyone to meet them at St .John's Hospital on Long Island

He had lost his cool at first, but the ghetto star was back in control. He looked over at Karen and smiled. "Breathe baby, just breathe."

He was about to be a father again.

CHAPTER NINETEEN

"I can please myself, like nobody else, I can touch myself. I don't need your help – let me do it miiiiiiiy waaay—I can please myself!"

Through their distribution deal with Def Jam, Loud Mouth Records was able to release the Dimes first single, *I Can Please Myself* with no problem. With this song, Tee and Toy were able to express their independence and their ability to tend to their own needs. Nationwide, the record instantly became an anthem for the ladies.

"I can touch me there, touch me anywhere, you can disappear, I don't need you here – let me do it miiiiiiiiiiy waaay – I can please myself!"

Wild Blood was happy that his first act was off to a good start, but what he was really looking for was longevity. So, the President of Loud Mouth made sure that Dimes stayed in the studio.

Tee, who was the youngest sister, was laid back so Wild Blood didn't have to worry about her, but Toy was a different story. While both sisters clearly enjoyed recording in the studio, the Loud Mouth staff learned from day one that Toylin would be a problem. Toy had the appearance of an Angel, but it was almost as if she had a split personality. One day she walked into the studio an hour late for a session and Vinnie gave her the third-degree for keeping everybody waiting.

"I'm sorry, Vinnie. I had to take care of something," Toy said innocently in her sweet voice.

In his new role as Vice President, Vinnie felt a need to put his foot down to sort of show Toy who was running the show, so he continued to admonish her.

Until she flipped.

"I said I was fucking sorry. Shut the fuck up already, damn!" Toy screamed.

Everybody in the studio had their mouths wide open in shock, including Vinnie.

Another problem they had with Toy was that every now and then she would have one drink too many. When ole' girl got drunk, she simply didn't give a fuck about nothing.

Wild Blood wanted to protect his investment, and he decided to personally keep a close eye on both Tee and Toy.

Within 30 days, *Laugh Now Cry Later* had sold more units than almost any other mixtape in Loud Mouth's catalogue. Makavelli was doing shows and making guest appearances while at the same time working on his debut album. Willie Black failed to respond to Makavelli's open challenge so the streets were under the impression that the 4-1-0 Hustlers had graciously bowed out.

Little did they know, Willie Black and the 4-1-0 Hustlers weren't even in the country. Roy Clayton, a well-known promoter, had booked 4-1-0 Hustlers as an opening act for a famous old-school rap group touring in Germany.

Willie Black was able to travel and make a little extra cash at the same time. Besides the money that Roy Clayton was paying them, the 4-1-0 Hustlers were burning and selling their mixtapes like hot cakes. This was Willie Black's first exposure to international fame and he was loving every minute of it.

As an artist, Willie Black was undeniably gifted, but as a person ole' boy had some serious issues! His number one issue was his inability to control his emotions. Willie Black would go from extremely happy to extremely angry in 3.5 seconds. Those that were close to him accepted it because they thought he was bipolar, and as such, his behavior was out of his control. Others just steered out of his way as if he were a drunk driver.

Nevertheless, Willie Black's inability to control self was definitely a liability, and this was demonstrated when ole' boy called back to the States and learned about the mixtape that Makavelli put out disrespecting 4-1-0 Hustlers.

Willie Black was seething! He was so upset that he refused to perform at any more shows unless Roy Clayton helped him find a way to record a response to *Laugh Now Cry Later*. Roy Clayton refused to change directions in the middle of a tour because of some petty beef thousands of miles away. As a result, Willie Black, in the middle of a temper tantrum, caught the next plane smoking back to New York.

Cub was upset by his partner's erratic behavior, but at the same time he was eager to defend the 4-1-0 Hustlers' reputation.

$$$

From the airport they drove straight to the studio of an old friend, Ruff Da Legendary. Ruff was one of the most underrated producers in the game, but ole' boy was about his business. He didn't charge a ransom for his services and he really didn't care about receiving credit. Ruff Da Legendary simply enjoyed making music.

When they entered the studio Willie Black demanded to hear *Laugh Now Cry Later!* After Ruff dug the mixtapes out and played it repeatedly for the duo, it was time to get to work. Ruff had actually anticipated this moment and he had already constructed a game plan. As Willie Black and Cub listened to what was laid out before them, they played around with their own ideas and put verses together in their heads without ever lifting a pen. At the end of the day, their combined efforts could only be described as brilliant.

Shit was about to hit the fan because the 4-1-0 Hustlers were back, and they were going super hard!

In the opening segment of the mixtape, Ruff had that old Michael Jackson song playing in the background, *'Everybody starting something, got to be starting something...'*

And Willie Black and Cub were clowning!

Willie Black: "Chandar is a faggot!"

Cub: "Yeah, yeah!"

Willie Black: "Wild Blood is a maggot!"

Cub: "Yeah, yeah!"

Willie Black: "We on automatic!"

Cub: Yeah, yeah!"

Willie Black: "Hold up, hold up, stop da fuckin' music!"

The record scratched and the music stopped playing.

Cub: "What you doing, my nigga?"

Willie Black: "We can't do no shit like this!"

Cub: "What you talking 'bout'?"

Willie Black: These niggaz are killers!"

Cub: Stop playing!"

Willie Black: "But these niggaz go hard!"

Cub: "Stop Playing!"

Willie Black: "Dawg, these niggaz are from the street!"

Cub: "I said cut that shit out! Fuck these niggaz! Let's go in and get this shit over with.

At that point Ruff Da Legendary dropped a hard-ass beat and Willie Black went in.

That nigga Chandar whole squad's finito/ the nigga Jerry Moore got hit with the RICO/

Word on the street is that they think shit sweet, yo!/ And I ain't spreading rumors I'm just tryna eat, yo!

Cub: *Willie Black gon' crack?*

Willie Black: *Picture that monito/ the only crack I got is when I cook pedico/ somebody call the Dimes so we can have a freak show.*

Cub: *"All you Loud Mouth Record niggaz*

Willie Black: *Ma Ma Bitcho!*

And this was the start of some serious shit. Willie Black and Cub were right when they referred to Chandar's squad as killers. The question they should've asked themselves was: how would killers respond to blatant disrespect?

Willie Black knew the chances was slim that the response would come in the form of another mixtape, but he had already made up his mind to go super hard and he would cross the other bridge when he came to it.

$$$

Wild Blood, Makavelli, and Corleone were posted up on the side of Ajax Park half-ass watching the basketball game that was in progress. The C.A.B.B.A.G.E Tournament was in full effect and Chandar's team was playing next.

Jerome Smith was leaning against a powder-blue Lamborgini Gallardo kicking it with Chandar when a black Lincoln Navigator slid on the scene with its system banging. The S.U.V. double parked near the park's entrance and it only took a second before every one's attention shifted to the sound of Willie Black's raspy voice emanating from the powerful speakers. Chandar couldn't believe what he was hearing!

"I ain't a muthafuckin' blood, damn sure a crip/ I'm a 4-1-0 Hustler, Del Gib is a bitch/

I'm quick to pull a nigga card man, fuck Chandar/ Jerry Moore was killer but his homie a broad/

Gunshots to Makavelli, I'm a bury that boy/ have the maggots and the worms fuckin' marry that boy/ Niggaz tried to shoot me down, fuckin' carry the boy/

Now I'm back bustin' without nothing to lose/ I'm going hard like a nigga still hustle for shoes – "

Suddenly, the sound of automatic gunfire sent the occupants of Ajax Park into pandemonium.

People hit the ground, people ran, people jumped into cars and tires screeched as they burned rubber fleeing the scene.

But Willie Black's voice remained, escaping from the system of the bullet riddled Navigator.

"I reach for the toast quick, grind for the cheese hard/ stay the fuck out my way I turn niggaz into retards/

How quick you wanna see God, that's all on you/ fragments of brain and flesh, that's all on you/

*my only regret is I warned your crew/ Now I'm a thug it
'till I die like I was born to do/*

That last verse may have been something like a prophecy because Willie Black pissed off the wrong people. Not only was his own life in danger, but any and everybody remotely affiliated with Willie Black was now on notice. Corleone just sent a message to any and every fool dumb enough to play Willie Black's response to *Laugh Now Cry Later.* Do it at your own risk.

Willie Black and the 4-1-0 Hustlers were now officially an endangered species!

CHAPTER TWENTY

It was like the demons of his past were pursuing him and there was nowhere to hide. Despite Chandar's strong desire to do good, he couldn't shake the eerie presence of evil that seemed to be lurking around every corner. And while the ghetto star did believer that a higher power existed, circumstances often caused his faith to waver.

"If there is a God, why is he allowing so much bad to come my way when all I'm trying to do is good?" Chandar often wondered.

These were the thoughts that resonated through Chandar's mind as he raced his Porsche truck through the back streets of Jamaica, Queens in a blind rage. He didn't know what had him more upset, the blatant disrespect that Willie Black displayed on his mixtape, or the inevitable response that the streets would anticipate from such a respected hood legend.

The truth was, Chandar still had options. The ghetto star was Chief Executive Officer of his own company, and as such he reserved the right to deal with any given situation with diplomacy. According to the rules of the streets, gangstaz and thugz were required to ride or die, but a business man's #1 rule was: "Don't take anything personal."

Nevertheless, Chandar had decisions to make and he was painfully aware that the streets were watching.

He pulled the Cayenne into the parking lot of St. John's Hospital and tried to think positive as he went to check on Karen and the baby. The ghetto star stopped by the gift shop and bought a bunch of balloons and stuffed animals before receiving a visiting pass and heading upstairs.

In the room, Karen was laying in the bed holding the baby while her girlfriend Jada yakked away garnering Karen's undivided attention. When Chandar appeared in the doorway, he was confused by the startled look on Karen's face. When Jada turned around with a similar expression, Chandar deduced that he was the topic of conversation.

Karen quickly regrouped, "Look who's here, little man." she said in a baby voice. "It's your daddy and he got a bunch of presents for you."

Despite the uncomfortable feeling, Chandar smiled and approached the bed to get a better look at the heir to the throne.

"That boy look just like his father," Jada said.

Something in her tone wasn't right and Chandar's intuition was screaming. He shot Jada a look, but she was smiling as if everything was the way it was supposed to be.

"Congratulations Chandar!" Jada said. "Karen let me get up out of here, I got bills to pay. I'm gonna try to get up here tomorrow, but if I can't make it I'll just see you when you get home, okay?"

Karen was shooting daggers at Jada. "Whatever bitch, don't call me, I'll call you!"

As Jada walked out the door, Chandar was holding his son's tiny hands doing a little dance, but mentally he was pressing rewind on everything that transpired within the last five minutes. Instead of Karen looking like she was happy to see him, she wore a troubled expression. And Jada's tone was indicative of a person who was being facetious.

Chandar knew that his blood pressure was probably up and he wondered if he was just tripping. Whatever the case, he felt a need to investigate, so without taking his eyes off the baby, he put his press game down.

"What the fuck was you and Jada talking about when I walked in the room?"

The question caught Karen off guard, and the aggressive manner in which it was asked told her that Chandar wasn't in the mood for games.

"Me and Jada?" Karen asked, trying to buy time.

Chandar shot her a look that scared the shit out of her because she was so used to him being sweet. Chandar's true colors were showing now. Ole' boy was a fucking gangsta!

"We wasn't talking about nothing," Karen said defensively.

Now he knew something was up. He didn't know what the fuck it was, but he aimed to find out.

"You see your momma playing games with me, little man? She playing games, yes she is..." Chandar sang in a baby voice before switching back to his press game. "Karen, I'm giving you a chance to tell me what the fuck is up, but if you're gonna sit there and play with my intelligence we're about to have a problem."

Karen knew he was using reverse psychology, but what if he wasn't? What if he really heard what they were talking about and he was giving her a chance to come clean?

"I'm sorry!" Karen said covering her face with her hands.

Bingo! Chandar thought before going in for the kill.

"You still ain't said nothing! You sorry for what?"

Karen's body shuddered as she laid there crying. "For" – sniff, sniff – "for not telling you!"

Chandar was growing impatient. "For not telling me what, Karen?"

At that point, little Chandar sensed that something was wrong and he began crying.

Karen's next words were enough to make Big Chandar's whole world cave in.

"I don't know if...if you're my baby's father!"

Damn. When it rains, it pours...

CHAPTER TWENTY-ONE

Big Time's gold Mercedes floated to the left lane and drove up the ramp at the Hoyt Avenue exit bidding farewell to the Grand Central Expressway.

Reggie Ransom and Barrel maintained a safe distance as they discreetly followed their prey to what they hoped would be a pot of gold at the end of the rainbow.

The Grim Reaper had been playing cat and mouse with Big Time for weeks, and now he finally had the drug dealer in his crosshairs.

After passing the West Way Motel, Big Time turned into the parking lot of Jackson's Whole, one of the many rendezvous agreed upon by him and his supplier. After parking he reached into the back seat and retrieved the black leather briefcase that was filled with enough Dead Presidents to initiate a new federal holiday.

"You need me to come inside with you?" Trey asked as he adjusted the 9mm on his waist.

Big Time glanced at the young boy in the passenger seat and smiled. Trey was a blessing in disguise. The young soldier stepped all the way up when Big Time gave him the chance he was looking for. Trey displayed the courage of a lion and the loyalty of a well-trained dog, and he was on call 24-7.

"Nah, I'm good Fam! Just keep ya eyes open and be on point," Big Time responded as he exited the vehicle.

From the opposite end of the parking lot, prying eyes eagerly followed Big Time's every move. The brief case swinging in his right hand did not go unnoticed.

"Road dawg, I think we hit the lottery," Reggie Ransom said, his eager eyes never leaving his target.

"What you think that nigga got in the brief case?" Barrel whispered. The suspense was killing him.

"I know one thing, it damn sure ain't his lunch," Reggie Ransom said. He leaned his seat back a little further. "Go up in that joint and order something so you can keep an eye on that fool and see who he's meeting."

Barrel was on automatic. He hopped out the whip and made his way across the parking lot into the diner.

$$$

Anthony Bennett was sitting in a booth near the back of the restaurant sipping on a steaming hot cup of coffee when Big Time walked through the door. The federal agent couldn't help but notice how

241

out of place Big Time looked dressed in urban gear carrying a brief case. As the street punk slid in the booth, Anthony Bennett didn't bother to hide his disdain.

"Why don't you just carry a sign that says, 'I'm a drug dealer and I'm here to buy drugs?'" The agent hissed.

Big Time was confused. "What I do wrong now?"

Anthony Bennett just shook his head, "Nothing Richard," he remarked, using Big Time's government name. "Nothing at all. How much money do you have in the brief case?"

Big Time cringed at the mention of his so-called slave name, and scowled at the agent. "Two-hundred grand."

The federal agent nodded his head in approval. Big Time leaned his head back into the seat of the booth and his mind flashed back to the incident that placed him at the mercy of Anthony Bennett and the establishment.

Big Time had just received an emergency phone call from Kool-Aid informing him that the spot was popping but they ran out of drugs. Out of greed, Big Time decided to drop off the last *big-eighth* of his supply to Kool-Aid while he was enroute to re-up.

Consequently, not only was he driving with drugs in his truck, but he also possessed $21,000 in cash that was to be used to cop the next brick.

Desperate to beat time, Big Time was racing through the back streets of the hook like a man possessed.

Unfortunately, a federal task force team was strategically spread throughout the area monitoring drug activity when Big Time's Cadillac Escalade zoomed through the vicinity. Unbeknownst to Big Time, he had driven right into a net.

At the intersection of 155th Street, a Ford Taurus drove in front of his truck and federal agents converged on the Escalade with weapons drawn. Big Time was guilty of being at the wrong place at the wrong damn time. As far as the agents were concerned, a young black male driving a $50,000 SUV through a drug-infested area had to be guilty of something.

While Big Time was being held on the side of the road the agents ran a check on his plates and searched their database to see if Big Time had any warrants. Simultaneously, Anthony Bennett was illegally searching the truck.

By law, after the agents ran a check on Big Time and he came up clean, he should've been free to go. However, Agent Bennett stumbled across the *big-eighth* of crack cocaine and the shopping bag full of cash that Big Time had left on the passenger seat. It was time to play hard ball.

Agent Bennett approached Big Time. "Richard Alexander, unless you can give me one good reason why I shouldn't lock your ass up, you're in a lot of trouble big guy," he'd said, placing the cold steel handcuffs on Big Time.

Big Time was speechless. They had him dead to wrong.

One of the agents familiar with the precinct interjected, "The streets won't be the same without this one," he said. "They called him the mayor!"

That caught Anthony Bennett's attention. "Is that right?" Agent Bennett asked.

"Yeah Boss, you're looking at the biggest fish since Jerry Moore," The agent offered. "Ain't that right, Big Time?"

Big Time looked as if he wanted to cry! His run was short, but it was good while it lasted. Now it appeared to be over.

"Let me try this again, Big Time," Anthony Bennett said in a low voice as if he didn't want anyone else to hear him. "Give me one good reason why I shouldn't lock you up."

The truth was that federal agents had violated Big Time's 4th Amendment rights because they didn't have a warrant or probable cause to search his truck. Anthony Bennett knew this, but he also knew that most defendants pled guilty to these types of charges all the time without putting up a fight.

For that reason alone, nine times out of ten they would get a conviction.

"I didn't do nothing," Big Time protested.

"Possession of crack cocaine alone will put you away for more than a decade," Agent Bennett happily informed him. "What do you know about Jerry Moore?"

Big Time only needed a second to think before seeing the light at the end of the tunnel. Ole' boy was on automatic!

"He killed three guys that worked for Chuck, and Chuck disappeared. Word on the street is that Chuck is dead too."

Big Time was squealing so fast the detective had to slow him down.

"Are you willing to testify to that in court?" Agent Bennett asked.

"Man, you tryna get me killed! Where I'm gonna live if I testify against the Big Homie?" Big Time wondered.

"We can relocate you." Agent Bennet suggested. "Or you can consider your other options: ten to twenty years in a federal pen with a cellmate named Peaches. Which do you prefer?"

Big Time silently weighed his options.

Seeing that he wasn't convinced, Agent Bennett laid it on a bit thicker. "We may not even need you to testify," he lied. "But if we do, I need to know that you're up for it."

To Big Time this was actually a no-brainer. The Feds were ready to give him a get-out-of-jail-free card in exchange for his testimony against Jerry Moore who probably would never see the streets again anyway. Big Time knew he was playing with fire, but his weak ass didn't think twice.

"I'll do it," he said meekly.

And that was the incident that placed Big Time at the mercy of 'them people.'

"Slide the briefcase under the table," Anthony Bennett said, casually looking around the restaurant for anything suspicious. "I'm giving you thirty this time; twenty for the 200 and ten on consignment. This may be your last shipment before the trial begins so tie up your affairs. Again, we may not even need you to testify, but we still need you to be prepared. You see the black Impala parked by the van?"

Big Time followed Anthony Bennett's gaze and acknowledged the Chevy Impala in the parking lot.

"I see it."

Anthony Bennett took a sip of his coffee. "The trunk is open. Grab the suitcase and handle your business. I'll be in touch."

$$$

When Reggie Ransom saw Big Time lugging the large suitcase to his Mercedes, he knew it was on.

This sucka-ass nigga is ballin' outta control!" The Grim Reaper thought as he watched Barrel rushing back to the car.

Barrel opened the passenger door and leaned inside the car super excited, "Yo! I'm finna get this nigga right now—"

"Nah Road dawg, get in the car and close the door. Hurry up!"

Barrel glanced toward Big Time's Benz before reluctantly getting inside the car and closing the door.

"You see how heavy that suit case is? That shit must weigh a hundred pounds. He got about 50 keys in that bad boy," Barrel estimated, his eyes never leaving the prize.

"If that joker got 50 keys, I can't wait to find out how much money is in that briefcase," Reggie Ransom stated calmly, watching the restaurant's front door. "Did you see the connect?"

Barrel was from the Country but he was far from slow. He immediately agreed that what was behind door number one, which was the brief case, probably held far more value than door number two.

"His connect is a black dude. Ole' boy is wearing a suit and tie."

"The connect is black???"

"Yep. And he by hisself."

The Grim Reaper went into deep thought as he watched Big Time's Mercedes creep into motion. Something wasn't right, but he couldn't put his fingers on it. A black guy moving dolo with all that coke? Nah, something definitely wasn't right.

"What we gonna do?" Barrel asked anxiously. He didn't want Big Time to get away.

"Let that fool go. We'll catch up with him later and make him tell us where all that shit is at. Right now, that briefcase is top priority."

Less than a minute later Anthony Bennett stepped out of the restaurant carrying the brief case. Reggie Ransom couldn't believe his eyes!

"Road dawg, please tell me that's not the connect," Reggie Ransom said, shaking his head.

A white Ford Taurus cruised by slowly. Two rednecks with police written all over their faces were breaking their necks trying to see inside the car that Reggie Ransom and barrel were in.

Shit just got crazy!

The last time Reggie Ransom saw Anthony Bennett was at Jamaica hospital. They literally bumped into each other. Anthony Bennett had a gold badge swinging from a chain around his neck. He was at the hospital to arrest the Big Homie, Jerry Moore.

"It's the feds, Road dawg," Reggie Ransom said, as he observed the white Taurus stop in front of Anthony Bennett.

Agent Bennett passed the briefcase through the driver's side window before glancing around the parking lot.

Reggie Ransom shook his head slowly, "Dammit man...that nigga Big Time is working for the feds!"

CHAPTER TWENTY-TWO

Ever since the traumatizing experience Chandar went through on Anthony Orena's private jet, the ghetto star was subject to anxiety attacks. The bouts began to occur whenever Chandar was in closed in areas or when the noise level was above normal. To subdue the attacks the ghetto star would place a hand over his rapidly beating heart and take deep breaths, willing himself to relax. Sometimes he would splash cold water on his face, and at other times, a cold drink would do the trick.

As Chandar drove out of the hospital parking lot he felt a panic attack coming on. He rolled the windows down in his truck. With his left hand on the steering wheel, he placed his right hand over his chest and felt his heart beating out of control. The cool air did little to help the situation, and Chandar realized for the first time that stress was the primary source of his attacks.

Betrayal.

Karen had betrayed him. He had allowed her into his inner circle and she betrayed his trust. Chandar wasn't one to put his hands on a woman but, it took every ounce of strength he had not to strangle her. His lower self was screaming for him to punch her in the face or slap the shit out of her but Chandar managed to keep his cool. He called her a bitch a few times, and thought aloud that he should kill her trifling ass. Aside from that, he kept his cool.

The soft ringing of his car phone was a welcomed distraction.

"Talk to me!" Chandar answered, trying to take control of self.

"Where you at, Big dawg?" It was Wild Blood, and his voice was filled with concern.

"I'm just leaving the hospital."

"Oh, damn! I know Karen is gonna kill me if I don't get up there and see my nephew," Wild Blood said.

As soon as the words left Wild Blood's mouth Chandar couldn't help but to think, *If it is your nephew.'*

Wild Blood continued, "Ayo, I'm at the studio! Everybody is waiting for you to come through, what you want me to tell 'em?"

"I'm on my way fool. Y'all be easy 'til I get there."

$$$

In the parking lot just outside of the Soul Convention, Chandar met up with Vinnie Garrett, who was also headed inside the studio.

"I heard about the mixtape," Vinnie said as fell in step with Chandar.

"Ole' boy needs to be dealt with immediately!" Chandar barked.

Vinnie had a good idea of what Chandar was suggesting and he quickly tried to change his mind.

"Chandar, I know Willie Black and Cub are out of order, but please, just let me talk to them. I believe I can straighten this shit out."

"It may be a little late for that, playboy," Chandar said as they made their way inside the studio.

Wild Blood, Corleone, Makavelli, and Jerome Smith were in the exercise room which also served as a lounge. Jerome was on the flat bench grunting as he slowly pressed 315 pounds away from his chest. Corleone was standing over him watching carefully, just in case Jerome needed a spot. Wild Blood ended a phone call when Chandar and Vinnie entered the room, and Makavelli could be heard snoring lightly on one of the lounge chairs.

"Wake that nigga up!" Chandar said.

While Corleone popped Makavelli upside the head, Jerome Smith sat up on the weight bench sweating and swollen.

"Big Homie, I'm not trying to crash your party or nothing, but if you want me to take care of that Willie Black situation for you, fo' real fo' real, I'll get at that nigga for free," Jerome promised, wiping sweat from his forehead.

Chandar sat on the arm of the chair that Wild Blood was sitting in and nodded his head. "That's one option Playboy, but there's too much on the line to make a snap decision so I wanna hear what everybody else has to say," Chandar said looking around the room.

Makavelli used the back of his hand to wipe saliva from his mouth after slobbering in his sleep, "It ain't no other options. Them niggaz is food!"

Vinnie Garrett raised a hand in the air like he was in elementary school, "Wait a minute, Makavelli. We got your career to think about. This is a business, it ain't personal."

"That nigga made it personal!" Makavelli yelled.

"Listen," Vinnie continued. "Willie Black is definitely out of order. All I'm asking is that y'all let me talk to him."

"Yeah, you got that," Makavelli said with a chuckle. "Let's just hope you see him before I do."

Vinnie looked around the room for support, and when he found none he appealed to Chandar.

"Big Homie, you're the boss so it's your call one way or another, and I'm going to respect your decision. My advice is that we don't do anything irrational. We can take a lesson from the Big and Pac situation. All I'm saying is it ain't worth it. Our hustle is going too good to allow something like this to mess it up."

Chandar thought about what Vinnie was saying. A part of him wanted to avoid trouble at any cost, but another part of him didn't want to let something like this ride. The name of the game was follow the leader—everyone would think it was sweet.

"You got a point Vinnie. But unfortunately, them fools dug their own holes. If you can get to them before the wolves find their prey then maybe I'll reconsider, but as of now, Willie Black is food," Chandar decided. "I don't want no responses to that nigga's mixtape. Not even indirectly, Makavelli. It's business as usual. And Wild Blood you keep pushing Dimes. If anybody wants to know about the beef with the 4-1-0 Hustlers, you tell' em, no comment."

And that was it, Chandar made the decision to take it to the streets. All Vinnie Garrett could do was hope that everything turned out for the best. In the meantime, Vinnie Garrett needed to find Willie Black, and fast! It was a matter of life and death.

CHAPTER TWENTY-THREE

Jerry Moore opened his locker and began dumping all types of commissary items into a net bag for Anthony Orena. He included brand new tubes of toothpaste, bars of soap, deodorant, lotion, and a variety of food items to help Mr. Orena get settled in. As Jerry Moore prepared the mafia don's care package, Mr. Orena was preoccupied telling Shan Will about the pre-dawn raid the feds conducted on his ranch-style home in Nevada.

"And then there was a huge *Boom!* Next thing you know, over forty FBI agents are rushing through my home with guns drawn. I nearly had a heart attack! So, I say to myself: 'Which ratting bastard sent the fucking Feds to my home?' My wife was there, for crying out loud!"

"I don't mean to cut you off Tony," Jerry Moore said as he held out the big bag of goodies. "This should hold you over until you go to commissary. You can use my radio too."

"Jerry! What is this?" Mr. Orena interjected in mock surprise. He pointed to the bag. "There's enough stuff in that bag to compliment six people! But I can't take it, honestly. Some of my guys are here, and let me tell ya, these guys revere me like I'm a fuckin' god or something. I haven't been here for an hour and already I have more commissary than I can fit into my locker. But, listen to me Jerry, I appreciate the gesture, you know I do. If I need anything, I promise I'll come to you first."

Jerry Moore looked at the mob boss with a smile. "I'll let you get away this time, but if you need anything, I don't care what it is—you make sure you let me know," Jerry Moore declared, sounding like a braggart.

And that's how the Big Homie would have preferred it to be. However, Anthony Orena was a made man! How could anyone forget the level of authority that the mafia boss assumed? Anthony gave new meaning to the word power. On I-63 alone he already had about a dozen flunkies. He had someone to bring him his breakfast, lunch, and dinner. He had someone to fetch his mail. He even had someone that made his bed for him every morning! An officer would never allow an inmate to pick up another inmate's commissary, but this clearly did not apply to Anthony Orena. He would send one of his flunkies to forge his signature and receive his commissary, and the correction officer wouldn't so much as look as if he disapproved. Anthony Orena was a Boss!

Although Jerry Moore always resented sharing "Big Boy" status, he had to admit that conditions had gotten better since Anthony Orena arrived on the unit. They were eating shrimp and crab legs almost every night, courtesy of underpaid counselors and correction officers willing to risk their jobs for some extra money or to win the favor of a mob boss. Staff members even smuggled in MP3 players and cell phones with chargers for the batteries. The only thing that couldn't be purchased by the mob boss was his freedom, but history dictated that even that had a price.

Jerry Moore learned that Anthony Orena was charged with ordering the murder of a police officer, and that his case was related to the crooked cops, Batman and Robin.

Although Mr. Orena was obviously in a tight predicament, he sometimes appeared to be more concerned with those around him.

"Jerry, listen to me," the wise guy said one day as they enjoyed a few games of Chess. "One thing I learned a long time ago is that you can't trust nobody. The best armor is to stay out of range...Check!"

Jerry Moore studied the board, then moved his King out of check.

Anthony Orena continued, "If you ever sit at a table to gamble, and you don't spot the mark within twenty minutes, then the mark is you! Check!"

Mr. Orena had a knight holding down his Queen as he maneuvered around the board trying to checkmate the Big Homie. Jerry Moore had a good game, but with the upcoming trial and all, he found himself distracted. Anthony Orena was taking full advantage.

"You're a smart kid, Jerry. I like you. If you never listen to anything I tell you, I need you to listen to this. 95% of the guys in here are no good. The way things are now it's hard to tell who's who. That's why I tell you, and you don't need me to tell you this, but you can't trust nobody... not even your celly."

Anthony Orena gave up trying to get a checkmate – or so it seemed – and he proceeded to march one of his pawns up the board. Jerry Moore was happy the old man let up on the pressure and took the time to try to solidify his King's fortress.

"My celly is a stand-up guy," The Big Homie said in Barkim's defense. "We were in the penitentiary together."

"A stand-up guy yesterday isn't necessarily a stand-up guy today," Mr. Orena schooled, making another move.

"You're talking like you know something that I don't know," Jerry Moore countered, as he placed his

King's bishop in a position to threaten the old man's Queen.

Anthony Orena smiled as he studied the board, but when he looked up at Jerry Moore his smile disappeared. "The case manager told me to be careful around your celly," he said. "I think he knows something that you don't know."

The old man moved his Queen to the square directly in front of the Big Homie's King and smiled at Jerry Moore.

"Checkmate."

CHAPTER TWENTY-FOUR

It was almost 8 pm on a Friday night in Green Acres Mall and people were rushing to do their last minute shopping. Most stores would begin closing about 9:15, so late night shoppers knew they needed to hurry.

Tee and Toy made sure they dressed casually so they could shop in peace and avoid much of the attention which accompanied their newly acquired fame. The group, Dimes, was an overnight sensation and their fan base was growing by the minute. Just a week ago Toylin went to get her nails done and couldn't believe how many people recognized her or wanted her autograph. Then, one day, the sisters were on Jamaica Avenue and a group of fans surrounded them—it was out of control!

So now, they took precautions and tried to stay beneath the radar. Both Tee and Toy hid behind designer sunglasses. (Toy opted for Prada while Tee preferred Gucci.) They wore their hats low over their faces. Their entourage included their cousins Kofi, Kesia, and Jessica, and two close friends of Tee, Crystal and Nicole.

"I'm hungry!" Tequan said as they passed an Italian restaurant. "Y'all don't want to stop and get something to eat?"

"Tee, you're always hungry. I don't wanna hear no shit when your ass start looking like Kelly Price," Crystal warned.

"Kelly Price lost all that weight, I don't know what you talking about," Tee said, dismissing her friends concern. She then turned to Kesia. "Keezy, you ain't hungry?"

"Tee, the mall is about to close and I need some shoes to go with my Chanel dress. Your ass should've ate before we left the house!" Toy complained before Kesia could respond.

"Yeah Tee, wait until we leave. We can go to Pasta Lovers. I need another pair of shoes too and I'm not trying to do this again tomorrow," Kesia said.

Kofi tapped Jessica's arm on the sly. They glanced at each other and laughed. They knew Tee was mad because she got out voted.

"Ohhhhh! Ain't that Willie Black and them?" Nicole asked looking through the plate glass window. Sure enough, Willie Black, Cub, and three of their homies were in the store trying on sneakers.

"Come on, let's go inside!" Kofi suggested.

"Y'all go 'head!" Toy said impatiently. "I'm going to get my damn shoes."

Toylin knew her family wasn't going to let her go by herself, and she was happy to see that nobody abandoned the group. She got her way again. She pulled out her two-way and began to tap in a message.

$$$

Kool-Aid had a new enforcer. His name was Damon. Unlike Trigger, little Damon wasn't ducking no drama though. He lived for the action. His favorite Jay-Z verse was: *'If I come back wearing a 4-5, it ain't to play games with you—it's to aim at you!"* And he meant every word.

Kool-Aid's Tahoe was parked in McDonald's parking lot on Supthin and Linden with all the doors open and the system banging. Booga's drop-top Z and Stan's black Yukon were in close proximity as the up-and-coming ghetto stars ate Big Macs and Quarter pounders while they stunted for the hood. It goes without saying, whenever the Dons play, the Divas are never far away.

While Kool-Aid smoked a blunt of exotic shit and talked business with Booga, Stan had a flock of hood bitches lingering around his whip. At one point, four bad bitches in a Nissan Altima pulled up next to Kool-Aid and Booga trying to find out where the party was at.

All the while, little Damon was posted up near a lima bean green Chevy Nova watching everything. The little homie was on point, and his interest was especially piqued when he observed a red Ferrari pull into the parking lot followed by a Platinum Range Rover. As the occupants exited the vehicles, a burgundy Toyota Camry cruised slowly through the parking lot virtually unnoticed. Everyone's attention was on the clique that just jumped out of the luxury whips. Even Damon was distracted! After all, it wasn't every day that he got to see a Ferrari.

While Chandar, Wild Blood, Makavelli, and Maxwell Smart diddy bopped inside McDonald's, Reggie Ransom and Barrel were studying the vicinity. The McDonalds parking lot was beginning to resemble a car show.

One of the hood chicks that was just sweating Stan went into instant groupie mode when she recognized the familiar face.

"Oh shit! Shameeka, that's Makavelli that just got out of that Range Rover!" China blurted out as if she lost her mind.

"Calm down girl, you about to have a heart attack. How you know that's him?"

"Shameeka, he got on the Loud Mouth Records medallion," Another girl named Dee Dee observed, then added. "I thought he was taller than that though."

Reggie Ransom and Barrel got out the car and was about to go inside the restaurant when the Grim Reaper peeped Kool-Aid in the cut.

Damon was on point now, and his heart beat quickened as he anticipated trouble. He inconspicuously jacked a round into the chamber of his nine and then waited for someone to make the wrong move.

"Road dawg!" The Grim Reaper called out.

When Kool-Aid recognized the voice he came out of the cut and approached the old head. They embraced like old friends and little Damon relaxed a little, but he stayed on point.

"What's up nigga?" Barrel asked, giving Kool-Aid dap.

"Ain't shit, Country! Fuck is y'all niggaz up to?" Kool-Aid responded with a smile.

"Barrel was just about to go get us something to eat and make sure the home team is straight," Reggie Ransom said, giving Barrel a look before looking around to see if anything was out of place. He made a mental note of little Damon laying in the cut, but he had already deduced that the young gun was part of Kool-Aid's group. He continued, "And I need to holla at you real quick."

Barrel jetted inside Mickey Dees to make sure Chandar and the squad was okay. Meanwhile the Grim Reaper got down to business.

"Road dawg, you know I fucks with you hard, so I'm gonna be straight up. I got good news and bad news, which one you want to hear first?"

Kool-Aid's expression turned solemn. He didn't know what the fuck was going on, but he already knew he didn't like it.

"You may as well start with the bad news. What the fuck?" Kool-Aid said, anxious to hear what was going on.

"Your ace in the hole is a rat. He's working with the feds, Road dawg," Reggie Ransom said sadly, as if it pained him to be the bearer of bad news.

"Who's my ace in the hole'?" Kool-Aid asked, but he already knew.

"Big Time!"

And for the first time in a long time Kool-Aid felt uncomfortable in the presence of the Grim Reaper. Partly because he knew what would be expected of him if this was true, and partly because he didn't think that he would be able to do it.

"O.G. you trippin'. You called good money with Peanut, but you're wrong on this one. I don't know where you got that information from but..."

"Listen to me," Reggie Ransom said cutting him off. "He's worse than Peanut. He's a hundred times worse than Peanut! I'm telling you, if I didn't see it with my own eyes, I probably wouldn't believe it."

Reggie Ransom explained to Kool-Aid everything that happened. He even admitted that his ultimate goal was to make Big Time come up off some of that cash. When the Grim Reaper finished presenting his proof against Big Time, Kool-Aid was devastated.

"Damn Fam, that nigga took care of me. If it wasn't for him, I wouldn't have nothing," Kool-Aid confided.

The Grim Reaper felt Kool-Aid's pain, but he wasn't trying to hear that sucka shit. It wasn't nothing to talk about. Dude was sour and that's all it was to it.

With perfect timing Chandar and the crew came out the joint carrying crazy bags of food.

"Come on, I want you to meet somebody," Reggie Ransom said.

While they approached Chandar, they could hear the hood chicks calling.

"Makavelli got groupies y'all!" Chandar joked, as he sat bags on top of the Ferrari and pulled out fish sandwiches.

"I know one thing," Maxwell Smart said. "The little dark skinned one got an ass like Angel!"

"I peeped that shit too! Call her over here Makavelli," Wild Blood suggested.

Makavelli threw a hand in the air and waved the girls over. Their gold digging asses left Stan by himself like they just found out he was HIV positive.

"Big Homie," The Grim Reaper said putting his arm around Kool-Aid. "This is my little man Kool-Aid that I was telling you about. The kid is a soldier. You know I don't fuck with a whole lot of people so he gotta be special. Kool-Aid, this is Chandar!"

Chandar wiped his hand on a napkin before shaking Kool-Aid's hand. "You gotta be a helluva dude, because in all the years I've been fucking with the Candy man, I can count on one hand how many people he introduced to me."

"Oh yeah!" Kool-Aid said, pumping Chandar's hand vigorously. "Out of all the years I've been

269

hearing about Chandar and Jerry Moore, I can't believe I'm actually getting to meet you."

Chandar took a sip of his soda and peeped Wild Blood palming the dark-skinned chick's ass while he whispered in her ear.

"Where you from Playboy?" The ghetto star asked Kool-Aid as he leaned against the F360.

"I'm originally from Buffalo, but I've been around here getting money since 1998."

"What you doing, selling drugs?"

"For real, for real, I'm involved in anything that's paying the bills."

"I hear that shit!" Chandar said with a smile. "You know anybody who rap or sing?"

"Hell yeah! I know mad people who flow." Kool-Aid assured him.

Chandar reached in his pocket and gave Kool-Aid his card. "My cell number and the studio number is right there. Give me a call and I'll set something up for you personally."

Chandar felt his two-way pager vibrating on his hip. He pulled it out to read the message. After reading the text, Chandar passed the pager to Reggie Ransom with a smirk.

It was a text from Toylin and it read: *Willie Black is in Green Acres Mall.*

CHAPTER TWENTY-FIVE

As a Muslim, Shan Will was required to attend a religious service every Friday which was called *Jumu'ah*. (Because of many people's ignorance of the Arabic language it was common for Jumu'ah to be pronounced, "Juma".) The service consisted of a two-part speech, or religious talk, which was followed by a group prayer. In MDC Brooklyn, this service was held in a small room that was normally reserved for recreational purposes.

Jerry Moore was just coming back from the law library when he looked inside the rec room and saw about a dozen Muslims siting in rows on blankets that were spread across the floor. At the front of these people stood Shan Will and he seemed to be speaking with a great sense of urgency as if something major had taken place. A guy named Kareem was standing at the door of the rec room as if he was on security detail, but when he noticed the curious expression on Jerry Moore's face he slipped out of the room and quickly yet quietly invited the Big Homie inside.

"You're right on time Big Homie, Juma just started. Come inside and hear your co-defendant speak. Shan Will is knowledgeable."

Without waiting for a response Kareem opened the door wide enough for Jerry Moore's wheelchair to get through. He was elated to see the Big Homie accept the invitation.

As Jerry Moore found somewhere to settle in he could hear Shan Will's voice boom throughout the room.

"There is none worthy of worship except Allah!"

Jerry Moore felt a chill go through his body as he heard the words and his mind digested the picture of Shan Will standing in front of the people as a Muslim teacher. He could hear the sincerity and confidence in the Little Homie's voice.

"Allah is the Arabic name for the sole creator, sustainer, and maintainer of the entire creation! He is one, without any partner or associate. Nothing is like or comparable to Him in any respect. It is He alone who deserves worship and obedience. There is nothing like Him!"

Shan Will began to pace slowly back and forth in front of the people, occasionally wiping sweat from his forehead.

"Whatever is in the heavens and earth is a testimony to His greatness and majesty. Allah is independent without need. Every being relies upon Him for its sustenance, yet He relies upon no one. He needs nothing. He does not require food or drink. He is the Sustainer without being sustained. He is the Giver of life and death, but He was never born, nor will He die. He will never pass away! He is the first and the last. He always was and He always will be. Glory be to Him!"

And so went Shan Will's religious talk. Jerry Moore was very impressed with his Little Homie, and although he was deeply touched by the message, the Big Homie couldn't shake the competitiveness of his own nature. He knew in his heart that he could become a better Muslim than Shan Will... praise his Lord better... give a better speech.

As Shan Will spoke, Jerry Moore began to imagine it was him in front of the people, but he imagined it to be a much larger audience. Shan Will's words became his own. As Shan Will went on with his speech, Jerry Moore heard the words in his own voice...

"And what kind of world are we allowing ourselves to live in, where 'doing the right thing' is only preserved through harsh laws and drastic consequences but not by voluntarily accepted principles? Is this the kind of world we want to raise our children in? If not, change starts here! Right here in this room, right now! And God knows, I've done some things that the devil would be ashamed of, but now I realize that Allah's plan is better than any plan that any mortal can ever conceive."

Shan Will looked directly at Jerry Moore as he made this last statement. It was as if he were speaking to him directly.

"We must realize this and familiarize ourselves with Allah's guidance. It starts here! Once ourselves are guided, we're in a position to guide the communities. Once the communities are guided, our families are guided, my beloved brothers in faith. They're placed in position to guide an entire nation. This is the kind of world I want to raise my children in! A world that is guided."

The fact that Jerry Moore was a ruthless street thug was unequivocal. However, change is always possible, and this was evident as Jerry Moore allowed tears to run freely down his face. The Big Homie was moved by the message that he heard.

It was a message that would change his life forever.

CHAPTER TWENTY-SIX

It was getting late but Willie Black and Cub wished their shopping spree could last forever. They copped Prada shoes from Bloomingdales, cashmere sweaters from Macy's, and diamond-studded earrings from Littman Jewelers. They purchased Iceberg jeans and damn near every flavor of Air Force Ones. Yet, they wished there was more time to splurge. Unfortunately, it was after 9pm and the mall would be closing at 9:30.

"Ayo! Let's jet upstairs and get something to eat before this joint shut down," Willie Black suggested.

Besides Cub, his homies A-K and Gee had accompanied him to Green Acres Mall.

"That's what's up. I'm starving," Cub agreed as they headed for the escalator.

Everyone carried bags full of merchandise from the various stores they visited. The mall was clearing out but there were still a healthy dose of amazingly attractive women out and about.

On the second level, the 4-1-0 Hustlers didn't play no games as they made their way into a burger joint and ordered enough food to feed an NBA team.

"Damn Boo, you ain't gonna show Willie Black no love? 4-1-0 Hustlers is in the building!" The rapper proclaimed arrogantly as a beautiful sister walked past his table.

The sister smiled politely but kept it moving.

"Conceited Bitch!" Willie Black yelled.

Shorty turned around and her smile was gone. She gave Willie Black the middle finger before storming off.

"That's all I wanted was some attention, Boo!" Willie Black yelled. "That's all you had to do in the first place instead of just ignoring a nigga!"

Shorty shook her head and kept stepping. The 4-1-0 Hustlers remained on the Food court, devouring cheeseburgers, fries, and fish sandwiches until they were good and full.

"Yo let's get the fuck out of here. I got some pussy lined up at 11," Cub said, standing up and belching loudly.

"Shit, I got something lined up too! I gotta stop by the studio first though. Ruff said he got something for us," Willie Black added before stretching out and yawning.

"I know one thing, your stink nasty ass got the cooties!" A-k said, touching Willie Black and letting loose a loud fart.

"Your momma like it!" A-K said gathering his bags together.

The crew were in rare form, popping tags, eating good, spitting at chicks, enjoying the good life they earned.

Little did they know, some dangerous people were vying to turn their good life really bad.

$$$

Reggie Ransom talked Kool-Aid into going on the mission with him. Kool-Aid was still tore back over the revelation that Big Time was no good.

"You said you had good news and bad news O.G. You already gave me the bad news, so what the fuck is the good news?" Kool-Aid asked as he maneuvered his truck down Sunrise highway.

Reggie Ransom was stone-faced as he reclined in the passenger seat.

"Road dawg, let's focus on this mission for now, and I'll tell you all you need to know on the way back."

Kool-Aid stole a glance in the old head's direction. "I know you ain't gonna do a nigga like that. You didn't make me wait for that fucked-up bad news," he noted.

With that, Reggie Ransom leaned up and turned the radio on. They listened to classic hip-hop until they were in the parking lot of Green Acres Mall. After Kool-Aid pulled the Tahoe into a space right next to 6A, the Grim Reaper stated the rules.

"Road dawg, listen to me, this is Country's mission. We're just here to hold him down. Make sure your young boy understands. Our mission is to make sure no one interferes – nobody! I don't care if the pope shows up while country is handling his business. Our job is to hold him down. You got that?"

Kool-Aid reached under his seat and came up with a black *Four-fifth*. I got you O.G., say no more."

Reggie Ransom opened the door to exit the vehicle. "By the way," he said before stepping out into the night. "The good news is, your ace in the hole is sitting on about 50 bricks. Make sure you get that up off 'im when you handle your biz."

And the Grim Reaper was gone.

This nigga got some shit with him, Kool-Aid thought as he walked toward 6A's Camry where three killers were huddled up plotting to kill.

The Old Head did all the talking. He explained how he wanted it to go down. Kool-Aid was surprised to learn that their target was Willie Black the mixtape legend, but little Damon was amped up. He was ready to put in work and he couldn't care less who the victim was.

The last part of the plan was actually a big disappointment to Kool-Aid—he was designated to stay in the truck with the engine running to assure a quick getaway. That was fucked up, Kool-Aid thought. But somebody had to do it. Kool-Aid reiterated to Little Damon that the plan was to let Country do his thing, and then he watched as the predators left to hunt their prey.

Inside the mall, kiosk and store owners were going through closing rituals as shoppers finished up their business and prepared to go home.

Reggie Ransom, Little Damon, and Barrel strolled through the corridor looking through the giant plate glass windows of the different businesses in the mall, searching for their target. Their only hope was that Willie Black did not leave the building.

$$$

"Shawty, I can't even remember where we parked at," Gee said, strategizing the best way to carry all the stuff he bought.

"We gotta go out on the Macy's side," Willie Black recalled. "If your head was a little bit bigger Gee, you'd be a lil' bit dumber!"

Cub and A-K got a good laugh out of that.

"Ha, ha, ha, Black, you a real comedian. If you was a little smarter you would've made it to the second grade," Gee bust back, putting one of his bags on top of the bags Willie Black was already carrying.

"What the fuck is you doing man?!" Willie Black shouted.

"Chill shawty, carry that for me."

$$$

They scoured the entire lower level but Willie Black was nowhere to be found. Country was ready to give up hope, but the Grim Reaper suggested they check the second level before aborting the mission.

As they stepped aboard the escalator and began to ascend, Barrel's face suddenly changed. He growled low like a lion as his eyes narrowed into slits of danger.

He had spotted Willie Black!

Willie Black and the 4-1-0 Hustlers, were stepping on the escalator on the opposite side to descend to the lower level. Reggie Ransom tapped little Damon in a gesture to advise the young gee to get on point.

When Willie Black was just about parallel on his way past his assailant, Green Acres Mall erupted into chaos!

Country raised the gun at point-blank range and let it bark! 17 shots rang out! Shopping bags filled with merchandise went flying in different directions, people dove off the escalator screaming while scurrying to safety. Others weren't so lucky, and were trampled in the fracas. Through it all, Country kept firing, sending paths of lightning all through the mall.

In the end, some eyewitness accounts would be exaggerated making the total amount of shots fired in the neighborhood of 40 or 50 rounds.

Nevertheless, at least 7 slugs found their mark, one being a head shot.

The mission was complete and counted as successful.

Willie Black was left for dead.

CHAPTER TWENTY-SEVEN

Chandar had a lot on his mind! He was in the private gym of his mini-mansion out on Long Island and he just completed a 40-minute cardio workout. The ghetto star did his best thinking when his adrenaline was pumped up, and that quick work out did the trick. He was able to meditate on his situation with Karen, and he came to the conclusion that he would take a blood test immediately. If the baby was, in fact, his child, Chandar was prepared to be the best father he could be. However, if the test proved he wasn't the father, Chandar was preparing himself to take the whole situation as a learning experience with the golden rule being—*Beware of the wolf wearing sheep's clothing.*

The ghetto star smiled as he heard Jay-Z singing in his ear, '*If you're having girl problems I feel bad for you son, I got 99 problems but a bitch ain't one.*'

"Yeah, right!" Chandar thought. He trusted Karen, and her pretty little ass rocked him right to sleep. *Never again*, was Chandar's vow.

Still, he resolved to handle the situation like a boss. He was going to sit down with Karen and talk it out. He wanted an explanation for Karen's actions, and he wanted her to understand why they would never get back together.

As Chandar relaxed under a steaming hot shower his thoughts turned to Jerry Moore.

Damn. The trial was less than 2 weeks away! Reggie Ransom had failed to find Denise, and her trifling ass was scheduled to testify against the Big Homie. Chandar knew that bitch was a snake, but Jerry Moore didn't take heed and now he was forced to learn the hard way.

Chandar's thoughts were interrupted by the insistent beeps of his security cam. He shut the shower down and grabbed a towel as he flicked on the security monitor suspended on the wall.

"What the fuck?" Chandar muttered as he watched two sheriff deputies standing at the front gate looking around the property. Chandar pressed a button activating the intercom system. "You guys looking for anybody in particular?" He asked, startling the two officers of the law.

"I reckon we are," the sheriff said looking into the cam. He consulted the paper in his hand. "We're looking for one, Chandar Grant, general manager of Big Red International Trust."

Chandar grabbed his terry cloth robe, "Well I reckon you're in luck, Sheriff. I'm Chandar Grant."

"Then I reckon I am in luck. Do you mind if we come inside and speak to you for a minute?"

Chandar started to tell him that he could hear him just fine over the intercom, but he decided not to play games with 'them people'. He buzzed them in and made his way downstairs.

When he opened the door he could see the officers marching up the path as if they had some serious business to settle. At the door the sheriff handed Chandar a document.

"This here is your notice, Mr. Grant. You have 30 days to clear your belongings off this property. This house is now the property of Marshal Irrevocable Trust, and I reckon you have five vehicles that belong to the Trust also."

The Sheriff was still speaking but Chandar felt as if he was about to have a panic attack.

"Whoa, whoa, whoa! This is some kind of mistake! This house belongs to Big Red International, I manage the Trust that owns this property!"

"We understand that, Mr. Grant, but you'll have to take that up with the trustees. I'm just doing my job. Now if you would kindly open the large gates so our tow trucks can confiscate the vehicles."

"Oh hell no! You're not taking my shit nowhere! Let me call my lawyer, he'll clear this up."

"Mr. Grant, we can do this the easy way or the hard way, it makes no difference to me. You have a copy of the warrant in your hand. If you fight us you'll be calling your lawyer from the county jail. However, if you kindly open the gates so we can do our job, I can care less who you call. You're free to do whatever you wish."

Chandar couldn't believe what was happening, but the voice of reason was telling him to keep his cool.

While the Sheriff's Department worked repossessing his vehicles, Chandar was working the phone trying to locate Charles Watlington. Unable to contact Charles Watlington, Chandar punched the air in rage. Somebody was playing a dangerous game, and at the end of the day that somebody would have to pay. That was the promise that Chandar made.

His phone rang. He looked at the screen and saw that it was Ms. Cynthia. Chandar willed himself to relax as he took the call, but Ms. Cynthia's first words almost sent the ghetto star over the edge.

"Chandar! The Sheriff's department is here. They said we have to get out of the house!"

$$$

Chandar had called Infra-red to come scoop him up. He was just leaving the house when Jada pulled up in her white SC430 Lexus Coupe.

Jada tapped her horn twice to get Chandar's attention. Infra-red stopped the car and Chandar hopped out. As he approached the driver's side of the Lex, Jada waved him around to the passenger side. Chandar's reluctance was testimony that the ghetto star was not in the mood for drama.

"What's on your mind Jada?" Chandar asked as he slid into the passenger seat.

"Chandar, I just wanted to say that I'm sorry about what happened, but it's not the way you think it is."

Chandar remained silent and avoided eye contact.

"By the time Karen got involved with you, she had already been intimate with Blueberry Loc. And by the time she realized she was pregnant, the two of you had already developed a bond, and she was scared to tell you about the possibility of Blueberry Loc being the father because she didn't want to mess up what y'all had," Jada explained.

Chandar looked at Jada now with a mixture of shock and amazement. Jada misread the look and continued to plead the case.

"Chandar, on everything I love, after y'all hooked up it was all about you. She cut off all communication with Blueberry Loc. Their relationship wasn't serious to begin with."

"Blueberry Loc?" Chandar spit. "Blueberry Loc? You mean to tell me that ole' girl might have brought Kevin Cook's seed into this world? The same busta that got my homie confined to a wheelchair?"

"It was before you Chandar! She wanted – "

"She wanted what, Jada? She got what she wanted! She wanted to rock a nigga to sleep and she got that! She wanted me to believe that was my baby when all along her trifling ass was sleeping with the enemy!" Chandar fumed. "She got that! Fuck that bitch and her motherfucking baby!"

Jada knew Chandar was a cold-blooded gangsta but she never saw this part of him. She knew he had a right to be upset but she still felt compelled to at least try to help her friend.

"Chandar she loves you!"

"Listen Jada, I don't have time for this right now," Chandar responded opening the car door to leave.

"Chandar, wait!" Jada pleaded. When Chandar turned to face her, she handed him a card from the hospital.

"At least take the blood test to see if little Chandar is yours. That's the name and number of the doctor you have to see. He's expecting you."

Chandar took the card and shut the car door without saying a word. He jumped in Infra-red's Bentley GT and they got ghost.

CHAPTER TWENTY-EIGHT

Kool-Aid waited until after the sun set before calling Big Time. As expected, the so-called mayor was laying up with a chick, but he insisted that Kool-Aid stop by the crib.

Kool-Aid was still thinking about all the things the Grim Reaper told him. He was still puzzled by all the 'Star in the Mirror' talk, it was like something straight out of an espionage movie.

Nevertheless, if what the O.G. had told him was true, then Big Time would have to die.

Kool-Aid parked his truck on the block behind Big Time's house and grabbed the Four-Fifth out from under the seat. He tucked the heat in his waist and slowly made his way to his destination to handle his B.I.

As he always did when Kool-Aid was on his way, Big Time left the side door unlocked. Kool-Aid slipped inside quietly. The sound of a television on inside the house reminded him of the hundreds of other times that his presence was welcomed in this home. Yet, this time was different. There was a great possibility that this would be Kool-Aid's last time in this house. Big Time's too.

Kool-Aid walked up the three steps that led to the kitchen and was keenly aware of things that he normally wouldn't notice. One of the cabinets was open, a frying pan with dried up lard glazing its surface sat atop the stove, and the refrigerator was humming loudly. Kool-Aid made his way into the living room and the cat crept up on him, rubbing against his legs. Kool-Aid gave a swift powerful kick sending the cat airborne, causing the clock to fall off the wall.

"Kool-Aid, that's you?" Big Time yelled.

Kool-Aid adjusted his gun on his waist, "Yeah, yeah!" he yelled back listening intently.

"Come upstairs!"

It was time to get it over with. When Kool-Aid reached the top of the stairs he followed the sound of the television which led him to a small room Big Time used as a lounge. Big Time and Yvette were cuddled up on the love seat watching a movie on his 64-inch flat screen TV.

"What's up my nigga! You heard about what happened at Green Acres Mall? That nigga Willie Black got shot the fuck up, he's in critical condition," Big Time reported like a gossipmonger.

"Hi, Kool-Aid," Yvette said smiling.

"Baby I'll be right back, let me holla at my man," Big Time said getting up and stretching.

"Don't come trying to rewind the movie when you come back either," Yvette said.

"Go 'head with that bullshit, yo! Come on Kool-Aid." Big Time led the way to his bedroom and closed the door behind them.

"I got something for you my nigga," Big Time sang reaching under the bed. He came up with a bag that he dumped on the bed. It was four keys of coke! If what the old head said was true, Kool-Aid knew there was more where that came from, plenty more.

"Okay, that's what's up," Kool-Aid said, nodding vigorously. "How many we got all together?"

Big Time looked at Kool-Aid closely trying to read his eyes. "I gave Booga, Mike, and Stan three apiece. That there is what I had left over. Why, what's up?"

Kool-Aid smiled, "Nah, I was just asking."

"Oh! 'Cause if you need more you know I can make it happen," Big Time boasted. He started to put the bricks back in the bag for Kool-Aid.

"What I really wanna know is, who is this mysterious new connect," Kool-Aid said in a low tone. "And after you tell me about that, then you can tell me about The Star in the Mirror."

Big time froze, just for a second. When he recuperated, he picked up the bag of coke, placed it on the chair by the window, and began walking to his nightstand. The nightstand where he always kept a gun stashed for times like this.

The clack-clack sound of Kool-Aid's 45 was formidable, and it announced to Big Time that there was a bullet in the chamber, ready to blow! The so-called mayor stopped dead in his tracks.

"What you doing, Kool-Aid?" Big Time asked, turning around slowly to face his longtime friend. "At no time can you bite the hand that feeds you."

Kool-Aid shook his head from side to side, he truly hated that this is what it came to. "Who's the connect?" He repeated.

"Man, you want the truth? 'Cause you trippin' homie, I'm gonna tell you... I get our coke from Po-Po. The connect is a crooked ass federal agent, and he gets the shit for free so he sells them to us for dirt cheap. What you trippin' for homie?" Big Time revealed his truth as if everything was all good. In reality, he was trying to save his life.

"What about the Star in the Mirror? What the fuck is that all about?"

293

"Kool-Aid, that shit is a myth! The star in the mirror is a term Jerry Moore used to identify rats. He also called them the backward star because the word 'Star' spelled backward is what? Rats! The federal agent I deal with uses that term a lot because he's the one who actually arrested the Big Homie, and I don't know, but I guess he became obsessed with that shit. He said that Jerry Moore blamed the Star in the Mirror for bringing him down. When he asked Jerry Moore what the Star in the Mirror was, Jerry Moore told him that if you hold the word Star in the mirror he'll have his answer. You know, a mirror causes you to see a reflection backwards. That's what that's all about."

Kool-Aid nodded his head. He was actually relieved that Big Time's story was making sense.

"You still lied to me about how much coke we got." Kool-Aid threw that out there.

"Homie, I got thirty bricks of that shit, minus what's on the street and what you got in that bag right there. I always lie about how much we got, but at the end of the day, I keeps it gully!"

"Damn son, I knew this shit was one big misunderstanding," Kool-Aid said lowering the gun, "But let me ask you one more question... the crooked cop, the connect, how did you meet him?"

The answers to all the previous questions emitted from Big Time like clockwork, but this last question had him stuck. As seconds disguised as hours crept by, he looked at Kool-Aid with a jackass look. Thinking quickly, as Kool-Aid raised the four fifth, Big Time tried to rush him!

And the big fifth spit!

Two shots to the gut folded Big Time up. As his body hit the floor, Kool-Aid put another slug in his dome before quickly jetting to the door.

He ran right into Yvette who stood in the hallway with her eyes wide in fear. "What happened? I heard gun shots!"

When she looked down and saw the gun in Kool-Aid's hand beginning to raise in her direction she screamed. But that was all she was able to do. Two shots to the head at point-blank range silenced her screams.

Moving quickly Kool-Aid doubled back, stepped over his one-time friend's body, and grabbed the bag of coke off of the chair. He got on his knees, looked under the bed, and pulled out the suitcase that he assumed contained the rest of the coke. A quick peek revealed that it was, indeed, the coke.

The little homie's mission was over. He got low like a thief in the night.

CHAPTER TWENTY-NINE

In the days following the Willie Black incident the media was slowly but surely putting together the pieces to the puzzle. In the beginning the reporters spoke in general, with headlines screaming:

Gunman Opens Fire in Green Acres Mall!

But as the story evolved it became:

Aspiring Rapper Gunned down in Mall may have been marked for death!

Ultimately it became:

Mall Shooting linked to Feud Between Willie Black and Loud Mouth Records!

Ex-detective John O'Conner was on his third cup of coffee when a photograph in the daily news caught his attention. Next to the photo, the bold print read: *Co-Owner of Loud Mouth Records is Allegedly Co-founder of Ruthless Street Gang!*

John O'Conner was calculating as he closely inspected the picture of Chandar. Taking a sip of his coffee, he began to read the article:

Nassau, NY—The plot thickens as authorities investigate the shooting in Green Acres Mall which left one man in critical condition. The victim, William Brown, 28, an aspiring rapper from Annapolis, MD was shot 7 times as he rode the escalator descending to the lower level in the mall. Witnesses say gunmen opened fire without warning.

When Officers questioned Brown, after his condition improved from critical to stable, he responded elusively:

"Y'all know what the hell is going on…it's not about music no more!"

When asked to be more specific, Brown replied, "I don't have nothing else to say! I'm not a snitch!"

However, sources who wish to remain anonymous had a lot to say.

"Willie Black picked the wrong guys to mess with. The staff at Loud Mouth are street dudes for real," said one source.

"They went back and forth battling with words, I knew something like this was going to happen," said another source.

But a music industry insider made the picture crystal clear, "I think competitiveness in hip-hop is good, but we need to know where to draw the line… Willie Black should've never mentioned Chandar's name."

The references are to a mixtape Brown put out disrespecting the staff at Loud Mouth Records, the label he was dropped from a short time ago. Records indicate that Chandar Grant is part owner of the company. Grant is alleged to be the one-time head of the notorious Blood Gang set called the Nine Trey Gangsters. He has close ties to jailed drug kingpin and accused murderer, Jerry Moore, who is currently awaiting trial for charges that include…

John O'Conner put the newspaper down and rubbed his hands together quickly. Although he and his partner were released on bail and would probably receive lenient sentences because of their assistance in bringing down Anthony Orena, the crooked cops were still looking for a way to win the Judge's favor. John O'Conner had an idea! He witnessed with his own eyes Chandar shooting and killing at least one person at the train yards. That information had to be worth something.

Batman grabbed the phone and placed a call to the United States Attorney's office. To maximize the effects of his cooperation agreement he was going to tell the government everything he knew about the co-owner of Loud Mouth Records. Chandar was the one that got away, but it's true what they say.

Every dog has his day.

CHAPTER THIRTY

Chandar hadn't seen Karen nor the baby since they were released from the hospital. He was tempted to call to find out if Karen had received the results from the blood test he took, but he decided to give it more time.

All the media attention on top of the rest of the bullshit going on was taking a toll on the ghetto star. Lately, whenever he traveled he wore a salt and pepper wig that gave him a Don King appearance. He was no longer able to travel in his fleet of luxury vehicles so he opted to push a low key Honda Accord. If by chance he was recognized by the ever-present paparazzi, the ghetto star would bark a prompt, "No comment!"

Loud Mouth Records was under a lot of scrutiny but it was business as usual. Chandar advised Wild Blood to concentrate on putting out good music.

While the powers that be plotted on removing the ghetto star from society, Chandar was in the studio listening to Makavelli's soon to be released single, *Ride or Die*. Chandar felt that the little homie really had enough talent to take the label to the next level. He just seemed to be a magnet for drama.

Everyone sat around listening to the club banging beat that Makavelli rode effortlessly.

"Ride or die, live from B-K N-Y, no need to keep it on the hush hush, how I let the gun bust/ coming through the scene in the money green Porsche truck/

Pedal to the floor cause I love the rush, one hand on the clutch, other hand on the dutch/ steering wheel in my lap I could drive like that, what!/

I got my mob in the cut, whole' squad in the cut, you getting robbed in the cut—"

While everyone else was listening attentively, Chandar's mind was somewhere else. His thoughts traveled back in time to the incident when Jerry Moore put the beats on Kevin Cook. Ole' Blueberry Loc, possibly the father of Karen's baby. Chandar remembered Jerry Moore doing World Wrestling Federation moves on ole' boy while Lisa talked a bunch of trash from her apartment window. Lisa had the heart of a lion, and just thinking about her made Chandar feel alone, even in a crowded room. He missed his other half tremendously.

Chandar glanced around the room and his eyes fell upon Infra-red nodding his head to the music. Once upon a time, Chandar gave Infra-red the name Fire Blood after the young gee burned down a bodega that belonged to some Dominicans who were selling crack on Blood territory. How he earned the name Infra-red was a whole 'nother story.

Wild Blood, A.K.A. Kendu was sitting on one of the mixing boards zoning out to the sounds of the single. This was the first song that he actually got credit for co-producing.

Standing next to Wild Blood was Corleone, A.K.A 17, a man who wasn't proud of the number of men he killed.

Chandar shook his head from side to side as he realized the seriousness of the people he surrounded himself with. He had a mean ass team!

And then there was Lucky, one of Loud Mouth Record's top acts. He earned the name Makavelli honestly. This was the fool that got away with faking his death! Simply amazing.

But there was one person in the studio that reminded Chandar of the good that he did. That person was Jerome Smith, a rival Crip that Chandar managed to see eye-to-eye with. Together they were able to stop a lot of senseless murders and unnecessary gang wars. Together they were able to bring at least some unity to the community, and that was a good thing.

After the listening, Chandar prepared to leave. He had a lot of things to do, his top priority being to track down Charles Watlington.

What Chandar didn't know was that this would probably be the last time he ever saw his team. That's just the way life was, you just never knew.

$$$

A-Blood was on his way to a Knicks game at Madison Square Garden when he received the news. He couldn't believe what his friend who worked at the Federal Bureau of Investigations had just told him. Chandar was wanted for Murder! Not only was his homie wanted by the Feds, but over a hundred agents were getting in position to conduct over a dozen raids in an attempt to apprehend the ghetto star.

A-Blood told his female companion to turn the customized Van around and head to Queens. He'd been keeping tabs on Chandar, and not only did he have a good idea that the homie was at the Soul Convention, he also knew about that ridiculous wig he was wearing.

$$$

While Chandar walked through the corridor of the Soul Convention, Tee and Toy were just entering the building. As Chandar approached them he noticed that both girls appeared a bit shaken up.

"What's wrong with y'all?" Chandar asked, sounding like an overprotective family member.

The girls looked confused. They recognized Chandar's voice but the wig threw them off. When they figured it out they began to panic.

"Chandar, the FBI is out there! They're putting on riot gear like they're about to raid the studio," Toy relayed, looking over her shoulder as if federal agents were on their heels.

"Chandar, I'm scared!" Tee admitted.

Thinking quick, the ghetto star said, "Don't be. We didn't do anything wrong. The only thing we're guilty of is making good music. Listen to me though. Y'all have to go and warn Wild Blood and them. Let them know I'm okay and tell them I said Blood Rule, ya heard? Now, go 'head and I'll get up with y'all later."

Chandar turned around and headed for the exit. The last thing he heard was Tee and Toy telling him to be careful.

As soon as the ghetto star left the building he literally bumped into a federal agent who was carrying a photograph. There was a team of approximately twenty agents behind the first agent and they were in full riot gear. Chandar almost had a panic attack when he recognized it was a picture of himself in the agent's hand. The agent looked right in Chandar's face and yelled: "Get out of the way, F.B.I!"

He didn't have to tell Chandar twice. The ghetto star tore ass down the walkway and didn't look back until he made it to Merrick Blvd. As he was about to cross the street a black and gold van pulled up in front of him and the side door slid open.

"Get in!" A voice commanded.

Chandar never thought he would be so happy to hear that voice. He jumped into the van and A-Blood slammed the door.

"Drive!" A-Blood ordered the woman behind the wheel.

As the customized van leaped into motion, A-Blood reclined in a captain's chair while Chandar got low behind the driver's seat.

"You alright homie?" A-Blood asked after a spell of silence.

Chandar looked at his longtime friend and nodded his head up and down, "Yeah, yeah, I guess I am for now."

A-Blood cleared his throat. "Listen homie, I'm sorry."

"That shit is over, dawg," Chandar interjected. "I was the one tripping', fool! You didn't do nothing but keep it gangsta from day one. I was just hurt A-Blood, and I guess when you told me what you did, you gave me something physical that I could place the blame on."

A-Blood knew that Chandar was the last of a dying breed. The ghetto star spoke from the heart.

"I still fucked up," A-Blood said humbly.

"You didn't know! You couldn't have known. And look at the bright side, you didn't fuck up this time. Your ass was in the right place at the right time. How did you know it was me?" Chandar asked, removing the wig from his head.

"Dude, I never stopped keeping tabs on you. I speak to Infra-red damn near every day. He's the one who told me about that crazy ass wig. But you know I know somebody who work for the Bureau, that's how I found out what was going down. I would've called Infra-red to warn him, but nine times out of ten they got y'all phones tapped."

"That's crazy! You been talking to Infra-red on the low, huh?"

"Come on Chandar, we're family. Infra-red is the one who kept telling me to be patient, he knew you'd eventually come around. I'm just not happy it had to be like this. You know you're gonna have to disappear, right? Batman and Robin told them people everything about that night at the train yards. They're going to try to get you for at least one murder, and then you got this Willie Black situation."

Chandar couldn't believe what he was hearing. "Motherfuckin' Batman and Robin! That's what this shit is about? Damn! I can deal with the Willie Black thing but that train yard shit is a whole 'nother monster."

They drove in silence for a while until A-Blood's voice brought Chandar out of his reverie.

"Chandar, do you remember hearing about Big Jack from the Bronx?"

Chandar looked up, "Yeah, yeah! He pulled a Frank Matthews. He was the one who got bailed out of jail for half a million dollars back in 1991, and they haven't seen him since. Word on the street is that he disappeared with about $20 million."

"It was closer to ten million," A-Blood corrected.

"Nah, they say it was twenty."

"And I'm telling you it was ten. I barely had that. Close to ten million and a passport. I had just started coming back to the country when I was fucking with Jerry Moore. I'm that nigga who beat the feds, homie. I'm Big Jack! I did what I had to do. Now it's your turn. You have to disappear. In 5 years they won't be thinking about you, in 10 years they won't remember you. Use some of the money I'm going to give you and get your fingerprints treated. I'm going to get you a new passport and the whole nine."

Chandar couldn't believe it. A-Blood was that nigga for real, Big muthafuckin' Jack!

"This shit is crazy! You know I'm never gonna forget you, right?" Chandar said with a sad look on his face. "As far as money and a new passport, I'm straight. I just need a vehicle that can't be traced to me so I can make a few stops before I bounce. Other than that, you've already done more than enough."

So, a vehicle it was. A-Blood provided Chandar with a black Cadillac Escalade EXT. Chandar made a few last requests and instructed A-Blood on how to break the news to the home team.

Then, they parted ways.

CHAPTER THIRTY-ONE

It was time to shit or get off the toilet! The hours had turned into days, and days had turned into weeks. It was finally time for Jerry Moore to start trial.

The first premonition that the Big Homie received came about 7 hours before the trial even began. Jerry Moore had just managed to drift off to sleep when Federal Marshals rushed into his cell.

Jerry Moore shouted obscenities as two Marshals woke Barkim out of his sleep and whisked him out of the cell. Another Marshal gathered up all of Barkim's property, only stopping now and then to assure that none of Jerry Moore's property was accidently packed.

The Big Homie was baffled! He didn't know what the hell was going on, but he had an idea. He consulted his watch and found that it was nearly 3 A.M.

Less than 15 minutes after the Marshals raided the cell they were gone, leaving no trace that Barkim was ever there.

When the coast was clear, little Bootsie, who was in the cell next to Jerry Moore's, yelled through the vent, "Big Homie, you alright?"

Jerry Moore started to ignore him, but he knew that the little homie was just hollering out of concern.

"I'm straight, fool! Them people just came and got Barkim," Big Homie hollered back.

It was silent for a minute, but then little Bootsie verbalized what Jerry Moore already knew.

"That faggot ass nigga working with them people. He's gonna fuck around and testify on you at trial."

And sure enough, Barkim was one of 117 people who testified for the government at the Big Homie's trial. The trial itself lasted 22 days. The jury deliberated for 63 hours. There were 36 charges in the indictment.

Jerry Moore was found guilty on every count!

CHAPTER THIRTY-TWO

Chandar called Charles Watlington's cell phone for the third time, but again the call went straight to voice mail. In all the time that he'd been dealing with Charles this had never happened.

The ghetto star looked inside his wallet and pulled out the business card that Charles had given him. There was an office number and an address listed on the card so he tried the phone number and found that it was disconnected.

"This shit is crazy!" Chandar thought as he jumped back inside the truck.

He needed to contact Charles and he needed to do it immediately. He consulted the navigation system and located the offices of Jacobi and Watlington. Within 20 minutes the ghetto star was parking in the vicinity of the prestigious law offices. When he entered the office, a red-headed secretary asked if he needed any help.

"Yeah, I'm here to see Mr. Charles Watlington."

"Do you have an appointment?"

"No, but tell him that Chandar is here to see him. He knows who I am."

The secretary picked up her phone and pushed a button. A second later she was speaking quietly into the phone. When she hung up the phone she told Chandar that Mr. Watlington would be out momentarily.

Chandar was relieved! For a minute there he thought that Charles was ducking him, and there was absolutely too much at stake for that to be happening.

A middle-aged black man with a balding head and a pot belly walked inside the room and made eye contact with Chandar.

"What can I do for you, Sir?" The man asked, giving Chandar his undivided attention.

"I'm good!" Chandar said. "I'm waiting on Mr. Watlington."

The man rubbed his pot belly and let out a chuckle, "Well, your wait is over young man; I'm Charles Watlington."

Chandar felt light headed. It was as if his whole world was spinning out of control. There had to be a logical explanation for this, and indeed there was a logical explanation... the ghetto star had been bamboozled!

"Sir, are you okay?" The man asked Chandar.

Chandar reached inside his pocket and retrieved the business card. "So, this isn't yours?"

He asked, holding the business card up for the man to see.

The man looked at the card with a confused expression on his face. "Where'd you get that from? It certainly doesn't belong to me. I mean, that's my name and address, and I am an Attorney, but not a Trust Attorney. Why would someone..." The man shook his head in confusion.

But Chandar was gone! He stormed out of the office and called Gail Grey as soon as he was back inside the truck. Turned out, she had no legitimate contact information or anything on the guy she knew as Charles Watlington.

Gail demanded to know what was going on but Chandar hung up on her.

The ghetto star pulled out a bank statement from Bank Muzuho in the Bahamas. The statement had all of his account Information on it. Chandar quickly placed a call to the bank and asked to speak to the manager. When the manager was on the phone, Chandar gave the woman his secure account number and asked her if she could verify the balance of his account. Chandar was put on hold for what seemed like forever before the bank's vice president, Edward Tillery, came on the line.

"Mr. Grant?"

"Yes, I'm here," Chandar answered eagerly.

"Okay, I need to ask you a few questions to confirm your identity."

"Of course, go ahead."

"Who is the trustee of your account?"

"Charles Watlington."

"Good. And what is your security code, it appears on the upper right-hand corner of your monthly statements.

"45342-053"

"Okay. What is your daughter's middle name?"

"Tyis."

"Very Good. Mr. Grant, you have the equivalent of 12 million, 700 thousand, and 53 American dollars in your account."

"Yes!" Chandar said, pumping his fist inside the truck. "I appreciate you guys keeping an eye on my cash for me, Mr. Tillery.

"And it's a pleasure doing business with you, Mr. Grant."

Chandar hung up the phone and headed for the honeycomb hide out. He needed to pick up his passport and other falsified identification that would help him get out of the country.

The Ghetto star couldn't believe the drastic turn his life had taken without warning. He'd been through enough within the last week alone to make any sane person go coo-coo for Cocoa puffs. At times he felt as if he was barely holding on.

Nevertheless, all of that was about to change. Chandar was leaving all the drama behind him, and he had enough money to start a brand-new life. Chandar had a plane to catch.

He was on his way to the Bahamas.

$$\$\$\$$$

As a precaution, Chandar drove all the way down to Baltimore Washington International airport off Interstate 295 in Maryland. He booked a flight to Nassau and was surprised that he was able to breeze through airport security so easily post 9/11. The ghetto star's counterfeit identification and passport were undeniably top of the line, but he still wouldn't feel safe until he was actually out of the country.

He still had a few hours before his flight departed so despite his lack of an appetite, Chandar forced himself to put some food in his stomach.

Afterward, his conscious got the best of him and he broke down and called Karen. He didn't believe out of all people that she would be the one to deceive him. Ultimate betrayal!

"I guess it's true," Chandar thought sadly as he placed the call. "It takes a fool to learn that love don't love nobody."

"Hello?" Karen's voice came through the receiver and a spectrum of emotions shot through Chandar's body. He took deep breaths in a futile attempt at keeping himself together. "Chandar, is that you?"

Chandar was gripping the phone tightly and Karen could hear him breathing on the other end of the line.

"Baby, I'm sorry...I should've..."

"I know," Chandar said cutting her off gently. "Listen to me, I just wanted to tell you, I love you – no matter what. Always! I don't care if the results come back saying I'm the father or not."

"Chandar, you are the father. The results came back today baby. You're my baby's father."

Chandar didn't try to hold back any longer. He cried. He cried long and hard, boo-hooing like a child that lost its mother.

"I know it's hard for you right now and I want to be by your side. Let me meet you somewhere," Karen pleaded.

"That's not a good idea, but listen to me boo. If anything happens to me, do me a favor and tell my son that his father was a good man."

"Don't talk like that baby, nothing is going to happen to you!"

"I want you to teach him Karen, and give him plenty of love, but don't shelter him Boo. I don't want him to get the wrong perception of life. Give him a chance to figure some of this shit out. It's in his blood."

Karen didn't like the way Chandar was talking. He was acting as if they were never going to see each other again.

"Chandar, whatever happens, I promise you I'm going to be there for you. And don't worry, your son will be fine. You just make sure you be careful out there, so we can be a family again. I love you, baby!"

There was silence on the line. Then Chandar said, "I love you, too." And the line went dead.

Karen held the phone in her hand and cried.

$$$

Chandar's flight landed safely in Nassau a little after ten in the morning and he made it through airport security and customs without incident.

The talkative taxi driver was babbling a mile a minute all the way to Laquita Suites, an upscale hotel that wasn't far from Bank Muzuho.

Chandar was preoccupied so he wasn't paying ole' boy no mind. His main focus was retrieving his money so he could disappear in style.

"Maybe I'll stay on the islands for a while," Chandar said thinking aloud as he enjoyed the tranquil scenery.

"You say something?" The cab driver asked, eager to engage in a conversation.

"Nah, I was just talking to myself."

The taxi driver laughed heartily. He caught eye contact with Chandar through the rearview mirror, "People tink if ya talk to ya self it means ya crazy. Me, I talk to me self all the time."

The island man was just being friendly and Chandar made sure to give him a generous tip when they reached the hotel. The driver was still amazed that Chandar was traveling without luggage. He handed the ghetto star a card. "If ya need to get around on this island—I'm the man to call."

In no time Chandar checked into a suite. The first thing he did was take a long hot shower. As the steaming hot water blasted his body he thought about what life would be like without having his team around. He knew he would miss his mother and his sister Pauline, his daughter Jasmine, and even Karen and their brand-new baby boy. He resented not having the opportunity to be a solid presence in little Chandar's life, but he also knew that he would miss Infra-red, Wild Blood, Corleone, Makavelli, Jeff White, Jerome Smith and A-Blood. They were his family too. Maybe one day when things died down he would be able to send for them back in the States.

Chandar stepped out of the shower and dried off. As he put back on the same clothes he made a mental note to do some shopping for a new wardrobe, but his first order of business was to stop by the bank.

Just thinking about his money caused the ghetto star to brighten up a bit.

In the hotel lobby the clerk at the front desk gave him direction to Bank Muzuho. He insisted it was only a five-minute walk, so Chandar decided to get a little exercise by walking. He would also get to enjoy the scene.

He encountered many smiling faces, vendors selling fresh fruit, kids running around playing, and birds chirping. It was indeed a beautiful day.

Chandar began singing an old McFadden and Whitehead classic from the 80's, *Ain't no stopping us now.*

"There's been so many things that held us down, but now it seems like things are finally coming around."

The ghetto star sang and inhaled the fresh air, and it wasn't long before he found himself entering the bank.

The air conditioner was on and it was a welcoming cool breeze inside the building. It was a small bank and only two cashier windows were conducting business. Chandar chose the shortest line and got in behind an elderly black woman.

"I know I've got, a long, long, way to go, where I'll end up—I don't know." The song rang in Chandar's head.

Chandar's voice was one that only a mother could love when it came to singing, but he had no shame in his game.

"You're in a good mood, young man. Good morning!" The elderly woman said turning around with a genuine smile.

"Good morning. Don't mind me, I'm just happy to be alive," Chandar responded with a warm smile of his own. He was trying to force all the problems of yesterday out of existence.

"That's interesting. I needed to hear that, thank you!" The woman said patting Chandar on the shoulder.

When Chandar finally made it to the window requesting to make a withdrawal, the cashier referred him to the branch manager because she wasn't authorized to handle such a huge transaction.

Chandar stood to the side and waited patiently. He was happy to finally meet the Vice President, Mr. Tillery, whom he had spoken with over the phone just yesterday.

Mr. Grant, it's a pleasure for me to meet face-to-face with one of our best clients. This is our second surprise today, geez. Mr. Watlington was just here an hour ago."

Chandar's smile slowly transformed into a frown. He had to be delusional. He could've sworn dude said that Mr. Watlington was just at the bank.

"Mr. Watlington? Did you say that Mr. Watlington was here? In this bank?"

God, no....Please??? Chandar prayed that Mr. Tillery was mistaken.

"He sure was! Come on, follow me, he left something for you."

Mr. Tillery led the way across the floor and through the bank's small infrastructure. They made their way into a room that was filled with safe deposit boxes. Mr. Tillery found the box marked 106 and handed Chandar a key.

"If you need me, I'll be in the office next door." Mr. Tillery patted Chandar on the back and left him alone, holding a key.

Chandar didn't know what would be inside the box, but he was certain it wasn't his $12 million. He took a deep breath as he put the key inside the lock and opened the box. There was an envelope. He tore it open, and began reading the letter that would send him over the edge.

Dear Chandar,

I've waited for this day for far too long. You think you've got all the sense. You think you can continue to hurt people and never pay the consequences. Well, it's time to pay the piper! When you had my brother William killed, I charged it to the game. I was willing to put it behind me and go on with my life. But, then you had to go and kill my nephew Kevin—I know it was you! He had a bright future ahead of him, and you took that away. So, Mr. Chandar, since you enjoy destruction I sent you my friend, and his name isn't Charles—It's Marshall! Marshall used your own greed against you, and he single-handedly stripped you of everything you worked so hard to acquire. How does it feel to know that you sacrificed your blood, pain, and tears for nothing? Lisa, she died for nothing! Jerry Moore, he'll be sentenced to forever in prison for absolutely nothing! And you? You have to live with it Chandar. Live with it or kill yourself! Either way, neither one of us can ever be declared winner of this game. I hope you're happy! May God have mercy on our souls.

Yours truly,

Raymond Cook

Chandar let the letter fall to the floor and laughed. "Ha, ha, ha! You got that, Playboy! We gonna put out another mixtape and get right back on," Chandar vowed, smiling.

Mr. Tillery came back in the room a few minutes later and saw Chandar talking to himself.

"Is everything okay, Mr. Grant?"

"Ha, ha, ha! Lisa probably on her way right now. She know that ain't my baby—I ain't stupid!" Chandar said as he walked past Mr. Tillery.

The ghetto star left the bank and sat down on the curb in front of the bank talking to himself. He pulled out the knot of money he had in his pocket which was all he had to his name. It was about three grand. He threw it all up in the air and shouted, "Make it rain!"

Chandar was mentally gone, or perhaps it was just a temporary breakdown. Whatever the case, the things he did in his past brought him to his present reality. Some people call it Karma, and others say it is what it is. Still, no one knows what tomorrow will bring.

We just have to wait and see.

Epilogue

Kool-Aid became heir to the throne in the hood! With Trey, little Damon, and Barrel providing security and eliminating any and all beefs, shorty was able to take his game to the next level. Thanks to Big Time, he had enough product to hold him until he found a new connect.

Infra-red and Candy became a hot item, and Infra-red, being the true gee that he was, stepped up to the plate to manage ole' girl's career. Infra-red ultimately sat down with Jeff White who used his pull at Colossal Publishing to help the homie start his own magazine. The magazine was called, 'Step Ya Game Up' and it was primarily geared toward giving new models a platform to take their hustle to the next level. Infra-red also started, 'Step Ya Game Up' management which gave him exclusive rights over most of the models that appeared in the magazine.

Wild Blood was happy to solidify his new role as CEO, only after A-Blood assured everyone that Chandar was indeed safe and sound. The Dimes blew up and Makavelli had the rap game on smash. The staff at Loud Mouth Records were eating lovely!

Willie Black recovered and was released from the hospital. Then it was back to business as usual. A well-known southern producer heard one of his mixtapes and flew him down to Miami immediately. Hours after Willie Black arrived in the M-I-A he was signing a seven-figure record deal. The hip-hop world was about to witness one of the biggest feuds in the rap game since Biggie and Pac!

Both Batman and Robin were sentenced to three years probation as a reward for their cooperation with the government. However, a week after being sentenced, the crooked cops were reported missing. It was as if they disappeared from the face of the earth, and as of the time of this writing, they were never seen again.

Anthony Orena was diagnosed with throat cancer and was moved to a federal medical facility in Springfield Massachusetts. He died before he was able to stand trial, and thus was able to beat the system.

Jerry Moore became a Muslim and was nurturing a healthy relationship with The Lord of All Worlds. He seemed extremely at peace, even after a Federal Judge sentenced him to Life plus 75 years to be served in Federal Prison.

Karen... she was indeed a strong woman! She missed Chandar dearly and vowed she would see her son's father again one day. In the meantime, she had little Chandar to keep her company and to remind her of her first true love. He was such an adorable baby, and he looked just like his father. It was as if Chandar wasn't even gone. Almost, but not quite.

THE STAR IN THE MIRROR

www.ingramcontent.com/pod-product-compliance
Lightning Source LLC
Chambersburg PA
CBHW071053250626
47159CB00002B/459